A LIEUTENANT MAX GOLD MYSTERY

LOVE HAS NO ALIBI

by
Octavus Roy Cohen

WILDSIDE PRESS

COMPLETE AND
UNABRIDGED

I

THE DOOR of the passenger elevator opened and closed. I counted four, which was about how long it would take for someone to walk from there to my apartment.

But my buzzer didn't sound. Way down the hall I heard another door closing and I encased myself in a shell of disappointment. I knew now that I'd have to wait an eternity for the girl I was in love with. Perhaps five minutes.

I glanced around the tiny apartment. It was neat as a pin except for the suitcase I'd opened when I dashed in from the train. I had showered and shaved and changed clothes and trotted out a half bottle of scotch, a jigger, a bottle of soda and two glasses. I hadn't had time to do anything else, nor any particular desire. Waiting for Dana was a nerve-racking job.

I was alone, but still the apartment looked crowded. It consisted of one room which looked like a living room, but had a wall bed trickily concealed behind what appeared to be a closet door; a kitchenette with a shiny electric icebox and an efficient four-burner-and-oven gas stove, a sink and four roomy cupboards; a sort of dressing room, and a bathroom.

It was furnished comfortably in a Grand Rapids motif: chairs that were made to relax in, a radio-phonograph, a gray-and-white couch which was roomy enough for two, a gateleg table on which you could place a modest dinner or a vase of flowers according to the mood of the moment, and—near the two windows which looked down on the street—my drawing board, across which were scattered dividers, compasses, ruling pens, triangles, irregular curves, pencils, hunks of art gum, and a bottle containing India ink. That was in case I got an inspiration when I was at home. I'm an architect. Massachusetts Institute of Technology, 1939.

Then the buzzer broke the silence. I hadn't heard the elevator door open or close. I hadn't heard footsteps in the gloomy hallway from which opened a dozen apartments which were duplicates of mine, plus a couple which boasted two rooms each.

I almost tore the door down in my haste to open it. Dana was standing there, framed in the yellow light of a discouraged ceiling bulb. She walked in and closed the door. I stood looking at her for a long time, and then I wrapped her up. She didn't seem to mind. I said, "You're twice as gorgeous. I wish your husband would let me marry you."

She walked past me into the room. She took off her coat and hat and tossed them on a tall, narrow chair which served no purpose other than to fill up a gap in the wall between the bed closet and the foyer. She had on a black dress with beige trimmings, and she didn't do it any harm. I said, "I wish I knew a lot of language. I'd start telling you how wonderful you look."

But I knew there weren't enough words in the dictionary for that. I might even describe her, but I could never explain how she made me feel. One look at her, and I got all full of emotions. Frankly and unblushingly, I was in love with her.

She sat on the couch and started to pour highballs. I sat alongside and reached out for another kiss. That lasted a long time, but since it was just a trifle after six o'clock in the evening, we didn't worry about time. Over the rims of our glasses we silently toasted each other and then sampled the scotch. She said, "I thought you'd never come back."

"Eight days," I said. "Forever. But this is worth it."

"Nothing is worth being separated from you."

I said, "You wouldn't kid me, would you, Dana?"

"About what?"

"About . . . well, you know . . ."

"Being in love with you?" Her laugh tinkled across the room. "How else can I prove it?"

"That question," I said, "has an answer. But it's the wrong one. So we'll let it ride."

For the next few minutes we acted like a couple of silly

4

kids. You'd have thought we hadn't seen each other for years. Every once in a while, I'd come down out of the stratosphere and try to remember that this was Dana Warren in my arms, *the* Dana Warren, the Dana of Ricardo & Dana.

The whole world knew about Ricardo & Dana. This girl was one-half of a dance team that ranked way up yonder with the best; with Veloz & Yolanda, with Mary Ray & Naldi, with the de Marcos, with anybody else you could mention. Toplining at the Club Caliente, grabbing fabulous money and choosing their own spots. That made it more than understandable that I should be in love with her, but nothing could explain why she appeared to enjoy throwing her affections at a big lumbering guy like myself whose only romance up to a year ago had been with an assortment of T-squares and triangles.

On the dance floor, Dana was describable. Here, in my apartment, with my arms around her, there wasn't a chance to make someone else understand what she looked like. To say that she was twenty-three years old, that she weighed 108 pounds, that she was five feet four inches high, that she had a lithe, slender, exquisite body, that her hair was nut brown, her complexion clear, her eyes big and gray . . . that was to give vital statistics which weren't important. It all added up to the fact that she was Dana Warren and that, by a strong effort at self-hypnosis, I could pretend she was mine.

Unfortunately, I couldn't maintain that illusion for very long at a time. I knew, all too poignantly, that she was the wife of Ricardo Sanchez, her dance partner, and that they had been married for almost five years. The fact that they hadn't lived together for the last four and a half years was gratifying, but it didn't bring our relationship any closer to a permanent or satisfactory basis. All we could do was to be together constantly and to hope that Ricardo would some day give her the divorce without which we couldn't consider matrimony.

We could hope that. But actually, we'd long ago gotten discouraged. Ricardo knew we were in love with each other. He knew that we were always with each other. But he had made it clear that he had no intention of giving Dana her freedom. There were reasons; perhaps the most important one was that she was the best dance partner he'd ever had, and so long as the act continued to rank with the best in the world, he didn't give three hoots whether or not she was happy. In fact, it had occurred to us a good many times that he took a sadistic delight in keeping us apart.

We continued working on our highballs, and slowly drifted back toward a semblance of normalcy. She asked about my trip and appeared to be interested in my recital. It was one of those things: conferences with Middle West city officials about an elaborate low-cost housing plan, discussion of specifications, speculation about the possibility of getting priorities on essential materials. It was all terribly technical and should have bored her to death, but didn't.

"With all those fascinating things to talk about," she said, "I'll bet you weren't the least little bit desolate."

I grinned. "I was, too."

"How much?"

I gave a demonstration of a man recovering from being desolate. I said, "Now do you believe me?"

She looked at me steadily. There wasn't any laughter in her voice. "Will you believe this, Kirk?—I love you terribly."

She had a habit of flooring me with unexpected moments of seriousness. I did a little talking on my own account, and we sat close together, shutting out all the rest of the world.

Then she was on her feet and halfway across the room before I could stop her. "I need a new face," she called from the dressing room. "I'll be back in a flash with some new flesh. We've got to be going."

I yanked myself down from the crest of Olympus. I walked across to my drawing board and started opening the mail which had accumulated during my absence.

It was the usual stuff: three invitations to cocktail parties, letters from a couple of lads I had known during my brief army service—before they'd put me on the politely-styled "inactive" list and taken me out of uniform; several advertisements, an announcement that an armory where I had once enjoyed playing badminton before the war was once again available to the public at certain hours. And a long brown envelope from my bank.

I glanced at the calendar. February 2nd. It was the

6

monthly bank statement. I opened it and pulled out some canceled checks and a long yellow sheet of paper with figures on it.

I wasn't particularly interested. But then I saw something and started to laugh. I laughed so loud that Dana heard me and came into the room. She said, "Let me in on it, Kirk."

I was still staring at the bank statement and still laughing. I said, "Look: If I were a rich man—instead of a poor, struggling, hundred-dollar-a-week architect—would you climb mountains and swim rivers to marry me?"

"That'd be an inducement."

"So we'd better do something about it, Miss Warren. I'm wealthy."

She looked over my shoulder and said, "What's the joke?"

"Those lads at the bank. They say they never make mistakes. I'll say they don't. Only once in a while." I put my finger on an entry dated January 28th. "Take a look, young lady, and make yourself respectful."

She uttered an exclamation. There it was, vividly clear to the naked eye: "January 28th—by deposit—$100,000.00."

Dana said, "I can ride along with a gag. What is it?"

I said, "My real balance is $726.33. They probably entered the hundred thousand to make me feel good. Tomorrow I'll drop in and kid their pants off."

"Then you didn't make any such deposit?"

"Are you loco?"

"I thought it might be something connected with your office."

"I'm not that important," I explained. "This is just one of those crazy things that can happen but usually doesn't." I looked at the final balance: $100,726.33. I said, "Let's have fun."

"How?"

"Just for tonight let's pretend it's real. For eighteen hours I am worth one hundred thousand dollars. We'll pretend it's mine. We'll pretend there isn't any Ricardo. I'll go to the club with you and sit through the dinner show. Then we'll go to a swank restaurant and make like millionaires. We'll drink champagne and eat steak. We'll insist on extra sugar with the coffee."

7

She said, in a solemn voice, "There is always a bleak tomorrow."

"Okay. I'll go back to being a poor man. But just for one night . . . why not pretend?"

She caught the idea. She always did, as a matter of fact. For one night we'd check our sanity and forget expense. I said, "I always wondered what I'd do if I had all the money in the world. Tonight, I'll do it."

"And wake up with indigestion."

"That's a horrible idea, and worthy of a low mind like yours. But we'll try it anyway."

She put on her coat and hat, and I grabbed mine from the hanging space behind the wall bed. I said, "I'll sit in the corner during the dinner show. On account I like to look at you. And all the time I'll be telling myself that in a little while I'll have you alone. That—plus my hundred thousand dollars— will make me feel superior to everybody else in the place."

We went downstairs and out the front door. The February wind knifed up from the North River and cut right through us. The street was frozen and desolate. The whole city still shivered under the blanket which had been spread by the worst blizzard New York had experienced in a decade. In the week which had elapsed, the snow hadn't melted. Tonight it had turned to ice.

By some miracle I got a taxi. We climbed in and held hands. I said, "Soon as the first show is over we'll go adventuring. Between now and then, try to build up an appetite."

The driver asked in a bored, patient voice where we wanted to go. I told him the Club Caliente. He turned around and stared at one of us. He said, "You're Dana, ain't you?"

Dana admitted that she was. The driver gave an odd sort of whistle to indicate that he was impressed. He said, "I got a kid that he collec's autographs. Would you gimme yours?"

She took a visiting card and a pen out of her bag. When we got to the club she handed him the card. He thanked her profusely. I handed him his fare and a big tip. He forgot to thank me.

The Club Caliente was on the deep East Side. It stood in the middle of one of those odd neighborhoods which is in the process of transition from slum to swank. It was flanked on either side by tenements which dated back to the era when they were known as flats rather than as apartments. The entrance was on the street level: the club itself was downstairs in what had been a basement.

Chris, the doorman, was shivering in the near-zero gale. But he smiled broadly at Dana and said, "Evenin', Miss," as he opened the door for us.

We walked down the richly carpeted stairs. Near the checkroom we ran into Ricardo.

He didn't look very happy. His handsome face wore a sullen expression. He glanced at us with obvious distaste. He said to Dana, "You're late. I suppose I can thank your boy friend for that."

She didn't say anything. She started back through the club toward the passageway that leads to the dressing rooms. Ricardo stood looking at me. It was the sort of look I didn't relish.

I felt an almost irresistible desire to hit him. But I didn't. Long experience had taught me to control myself. I shoved past him and went inside.

But I knew then—as I had always known—that things couldn't go on as they were. "Some day," I said, "something drastic is going to happen."

I said it to myself. Just to let off steam. I didn't even suspect how right I was.

II

Visitors to New York are invariably disappointed by their first glimpse of famous night spots. Because it's New York, they expect everything to be on a grand scale. They look for dance floors the size of the waiting room at Pennsylvania Station, a million tables more or less, and a lot of plush and glitter. The only thing they get that's bigger than their anticipation is the check.

The Club Caliente was the newest of the really top spots. If you were a member in good standing of the Cafe Society set—the sort of a dope who makes the rounds just because it's the thing to do—the Caliente was a must on your itinerary. Maybe it came first, maybe last, maybe in between. But it's there. It can't be left off the list any more than the Stork can be forgotten.

It had started modestly and bloomed like a sunflower. The manager was a smart lad who kept pouring his profits back into a venture which he figured had an excellent chance of becoming an institution. Originally a small room, plus bar, in the basement of a middle-aged apartment house, it had caught on with the name crowd and therefore had attracted the suckers who enjoy spending big money for the privilege of breathing the same overstuffed air.

The original room had been doubled in size. The decoration job was a honey: cream and jade and expensive and soothing. The dinners were excellent, the suppers good, the drinks sizeable, the service perfect. Show talent was always the best. The weekly outgo was terrific, but the take even more so.

The location was out-of-the-way, but that didn't bother the late crowd. The Caliente was one of the places to go—so they went. They went and had their pictures taken if they were important, or they watched important people undergoing the process and then got a thrill by inquiring of bored waiters who they were.

You could stay as long as your money held out. You could eat well, drink good liquor, buy silly little dolls and woolly dogs, pay outrageous prices for gardenias and kid yourself that you were having the time of your life. You could store it all up and talk about it the next day, which was calculated to make you important in the eyes of friends who couldn't afford what you also couldn't afford.

When I first met Dana Warren she was dancing at the Caliente. I got in the habit of hanging around, which, on my salary, threatened bankruptcy, but that didn't seem important when I balanced it against the prospect of seeing Dana. Since that time she and her partner had been to a lot of other cities and now they were back at the Caliente again for as long as they wanted to stay.

The arrangement of the place was unusual. As an architect

10

I could imagine the headache that some fellow-sufferer must have undergone taking care of the expansion which prosperity had brought.

At the foot of the steps was a checkroom and a sort of lobby. Passing through that, you swung back a heavy plate-glass door and entered the dimly lighted bar. There was a curtain between the bar and the main dining room so that the barflies who were not stuck with a cabaret tax couldn't see the show. Unless the curtain was carelessly pulled, which it usually was.

The dining room, with its orchestra stand and dance floor, now occupied all of an enormous rectangle which originally had taken care of everything: kitchen, rest rooms, dressing rooms and what-have-you.

To solve this need for more space, it had been necessary to lease the basement of the adjoining building, which was an ancient red-brick structure with two flats on each floor. Between the rear of the club and the next building, a passageway had been cut. It was a bleak, dreary, undecorated thing, badly lighted by naked bulbs which seemed always about to flicker out.

The orchestra stand was at the opposite end from the bar. Immediately behind it were the rest rooms with modest designations on the ivory doors. To the right of the rest rooms were the storerooms and kitchens. To the left stretched the passageway leading to the next building. Rooms opened from that passageway: offices and dressing rooms. There was a big room for the lovelies who made up the line, and individual rooms for the principals. Three of these latter rooms had private baths. They were large and comfortable, and you'd never guess that the building overhead was little better than a tenement. Under the fire laws there was an exit through the tenement, but the door which opened onto the passageway was kept shut. It could be used, but customarily the Caliente personnel came and went through the club itself.

I took my usual table near the bandstand. I had a good view of the floor, and I was near the passageway, so that when Dana got dressed and was waiting to go on she could sit with me. Except for sometimes on Saturday nights, I never had any trouble getting that table because it was a pretty bad

11

location and the customers didn't want it. But it suited me fine.

The place was about half full, which was the usual size of the dinner crowd. There'd be a show at nine o'clock, and another at 12:30 or 1:00 A.M. Dancing from 7:30 until curfew. Two orchestras: a sweet name band and a nifty outfit for rhumbas and waltzes. The cover charge was two dollars and the balance of the expense was proportionate. It was much too rich for my blood, but all the employees knew that Dana and I were friends, and they usually forgot to give me a check. They never remembered the cover charge under any circumstances.

The show was good. It started with the gals. They were young and beautifully proportioned and looked lovely unless, or until, you happened to look at their eyes, which were hard and wise and blank. There was a famous female singer. A suave young man who worked with a French poodle was one of the greatest comics I ever saw. Then the chorus again. And finally, the topper—Ricardo & Dana.

I ordered a cup of coffee, lighted a cigarette, and watched the show. I was having myself a grand time. Being away from New York hadn't meant a thing. Being away from Dana had meant plenty.

In my pocket was the long brown envelope which contained the bank statement. I was getting a kick out of that. I had visions of the head waiter wanting to know whether I could afford to be there. All I would have to do would be to produce the bank statement and say, "Look! One hundred thousand dollars—that's my balance. Now bring me a second cup." I wouldn't have to explain that it was all a mistake. Tonight I could prove I was rich, whether I was or not. And that thought intrigued me. It didn't matter what you actually had: it was what you could make people believe that counted. Smart me. Kirk Douglas, architect and philosopher. Clever thoughts *a la carte*. Fun tonight, just being this close to Dana, and fun tomorrow when I started kidding the boys at the bank about the mistake they'd made. I felt so good that I didn't even worry about all the young fellows who were wearing the same kind of army uniform I had worn for a year . . . before they had decided in Washington, for no

12

discernible reason, that I could help the war effort even more by being inactive.

The M.C. called for silence and made a simple introduction of the dance act. Ricardo always made his entrance from the other side of the bandstand. And now, as the sensuous music of the tango swept across the floor, Dana rushed in from the passageway. She made a cute little gesture as she passed me, and left me a smile to hold onto. Then she was out on the floor with her partner.

As I watched, I was gripped by an uncomfortable sensation which I never had been able to shake off. I couldn't look at Dana out there and believe that she was the same girl who had been in my arms an hour ago.

On the floor she was utterly different from the bright, gay, natural, bantering young lady I was in love with. She was different in every way. Her face was different, her hair was different, her expression was different, her clothes were different.

Tonight she was wearing a sophisticated black dress which accentuated every lovely curve of her exquisite figure. Her hair, which she usually wore informally waved back from her face and combed casually to fall softly over her shoulders, was now parted on the side and brushed off the forehead. The back was swept up and caught by a jeweled comb. She danced with her eyes half closed and with her lips parted. She looked passionate and seductive, which was swell with me, except that it was passion and seductiveness in which I played no part.

She danced with her whole body. The rhythm seemed to flow into her from the orchestra and to flow out through her feet. She was in another world—a world in which I did not belong. I felt proud and helpless.

Ricardo was a superb partner. Maybe he danced better than she did. I wasn't a very good critic. But out there on the floor, I couldn't hate him. He was perfection. He belonged in the upper brackets. The team belonged there. They held you breathless.

The personalities as I knew them vanished in the magic of their dancing. They were a unit. As dancers, they belonged together. They went through the intricacies of their tango.

13

The lifts were beautifully effortless. When they finished, there was an instant of silence, and then a wave of applause.

Their second dance was a gay, lilting polka and their third a novelty number which finished with a sensational lift and spin. The applause at the end of this was deafening. They wound up with a brief and delightful waltz, then took three bows; the orchestra swung into a dance number, and the show was over. I felt let down. I wondered why I punished myself by watching this night after night. It emphasized something that I preferred not to think about. It wasn't jealousy. Not of Ricardo, anyway. I could be jealous of him at other times. But on the floor it wasn't Ricardo, the man: nor was it Dana, the woman. It was perfection; a perfection in which I had no place.

Dana waved at me again and vanished in the chilly passageway leading to her dressing room, which was at the farthest end. I stayed where I was and fired up another cigarette. Then someone paused by my table and I looked up at Ricardo.

He was handsome, all right. Six feet tall, weighing perhaps a hundred and eighty, he had the black hair, tiny moustache, olive complexion and gleaming white teeth of the Latin. He was, as the head waiter had once confided, a smart cookie.

He had been born and raised in Brooklyn. He had come up the hard way and knew all the answers. His name was genuine, his father having been Puerto Rican and his mother American. He had learned a fair Spanish from his father. But he was too shrewd to build himself up as a South American. It had been his policy to publicize his Brooklyn background. He played on it so consistently that most people didn't believe him. They thought it was a gag. The Broadway columnists loved it. From a publicity standpoint, he couldn't have made a smarter move.

He stood looking down at me. He was a man now, not a dancer—and I didn't like him. That went double. He said, "You're back, huh?"

"Yes."

"How are you and my wife getting along?"

It wasn't what he said; it was the way he said it that I didn't like. He knew that Dana and I were in love with each

14

other. He knew that we were together constantly. To a man of his stamp that could mean only one thing. But it didn't seem to do anything more than to afford him amusement. He repeated his question. I didn't say anything.

He went on: "You taking her out between shows?"

"Maybe."

"You know damn well you are."

There wasn't any use answering that, either. He took out a gold cigarette case and put a little white cylinder between his lips.

"With me," he said deliberately, "she was always cold as ice."

He walked away. I hoped he couldn't see that my fists were clenched under the table. I was still that way when Dana came through the doorway and said gaily, "Let's go, Rich Guy."

I bought my coat and hat back from the checkroom girl for a quarter. We decided to walk. From one angle that was a mistake because the wind seemed to shoot icicles right through us. From another angle it was good because it helped sweep Ricardo from my mind. It helped, but it didn't do a thorough job.

We got to our restaurant at 10:30. We abandoned our champagne idea. We ordered steaks with mushroom sauce plus the usual dinner trimmings. I tried to keep it light, but didn't succeed very well. Over the coffee and liqueurs, Dana leaned across the table and touched my hand. "What's wrong?" she asked.

I said, "Nothing."

"Try again."

I didn't look at her. I said, "The usual thing."

"Ricardo been baiting you?"

"Something like that." I faced her squarely. "Isn't there something we can do about it, sweetheart?"

"What?" She was very patient with me, considering we'd been over it a thousand times. "There's nothing between Ricardo and me, but we *are* married. He won't grant me a divorce, and so far as I know, or can prove, he's done nothing to give me grounds for one. He swears that even if I went to

15

Reno, he'd follow me there and contest it. And he isn't bluffing."

"It's the act, isn't it?"

"Yes."

"Haven't you offered to go right on with it if he'd give you a divorce?"

"Yes. But he doesn't believe me. And also . . ."

"Also what?"

Her cheeks were pink. "He knows that I'd marry you. And he's afraid that if I did . . . well, that things might happen. . . ."

"Children?"

"Yes. He won't take chances."

The grim humor of it struck me suddenly. I laughed. "It's a new method," I said. "But it's certainly effective."

She thought that was funny, too. The laughter helped a lot. But it didn't make the evening what we had wanted it to be. It was grand, but it wasn't perfect. We worked at it, perhaps too hard. At midnight, I took her back to the club and said good night. We made a date for the following night. "But no steak," I warned. "Hash only. I'm going to the bank tomorrow and let them strip me of my wealth."

I knew I wouldn't sleep. I was thinking about too many things. I lay down on the bed and stared into the darkness. The next thing I knew the alarm clock was going off. The hands pointed to 7:30 and it was black as midnight outside.

I bathed, shaved, dressed, drank some coffee and orange juice, and went to the office. I reported to the big bosses. They seemed satisfied with what I had done. I spoke to a couple of the other boys in the drafting room and went out. Nothing to do until Monday.

I went to the bank. It was a branch on the corner near my office. I knew several of the men, including George Larsen, the assistant manager. He saw me come in and said, "Hello." I walked behind the railing and sat down near his desk. I motioned for two other fellows to come over. I said, "You boys never make mistakes, do you?"

George said he hoped not.

"But you wouldn't swear to it?"

"Almost."

16

"That isn't enough." I pulled the brown envelope out of my pocket and produced the yellow sheet of paper with figures on it.

"Feast your eyes on that," I invited. "Is that a laugh or is that a laugh?"

All three of them glanced at it. Then Larsen said, "What's wrong with it?"

"Wrong? Are you kidding?" I read one entry: "January 28th—by deposit—$100,000.00."

George said, "So what?"

"So your bookkeeping department is crazy. I never had a hundred thousand dollars in my life, and probably never will have. And if I did . . ."

Again the three men exchanged looks. One of them said, "You think that's a mistake?"

"Don't be absurd. I *know* it's a mistake."

Larsen shook his head.

"It's not a mistake," he said. "On January 28th we received one hundred thousand dollars in cash with instructions to deposit it to your account."

III

I STARED AT George Larsen and he did the same to me. I said, "April Fool's Day is a long way off."

He didn't say anything. Neither did the other two immaculate, chastely-garbed gentlemen who worked with him. They tried to keep their expressions impassive, but they weren't having much success. After all, a hundred thousand dollars was a lot of money. They looked at it all day long, but that was impersonal. When it actually belonged to someone they knew . . . that was different.

I said, "I give up. And I'm asking the sixty-four-dollar question: Where would I get one hundred thousand dollars?"

George smiled bleakly. "You might have held up an armored car," he suggested with what he fancied was hot humor.

"I didn't. I didn't make this deposit, either. I saw it en-

17

tered on the statement which was waiting for me when I got home last night. I came in to kid you fellows because I knew it was a mistake. I still think so."

"It wasn't a mistake," he said gravely. "So far as we're concerned, it's yours, subject to your check."

I sat down. So did George and so did his co-workers. We pulled our chairs into a little circle and somebody passed a pack of cigarettes around, forgetting in the excitement that there was a shortage on. I said, "Tell me more."

"There isn't much to tell. We were unusually busy that morning. A messenger came in and asked for me—"

"A uniformed messenger?"

"No. Just a man. I knew he was a messenger because when he gave me the package, he also handed me a little book to sign."

"What did he look like?"

"I'm sorry, Kirk. I haven't the faintest idea. I was all messed up with a lot of papers and three people were waiting to see me. It was a plain, ordinary, bulky parcel wrapped in brown paper. I didn't know what was in it or who it was from. I left it sitting on my desk until I'd finished what I was doing. That took about half an hour. Then I opened it."

"What did you find?"

"Money. Lots of money. Fifties and tens and twenties. There wasn't any sequence to the serial numbers—a banker notices that instinctively. The bills weren't packaged. It looked like money someone might have won in a crap game, if you know what I mean. Not new; not old. Nothing to make it look different from any other hundred thousand we might scrape together. With it was a note from you." He fished through a batch of papers and tossed me an 8½ x 11 sheet with typewriting on it. The note was short:

> Dear George—
> I can't drop by personally, and I don't want to carry this much cash around with me. Will you be good enough to deposit it to my account?
> I'll be buying you a drink next week. Until then—
> Bestest—
> KIRK DOUGLAS

18

I said, "Why should I sign it on the typewriter?"

"Why shouldn't you? It might be unusual, but it isn't impossible."

"What happened then?"

"I sent the money to one of the tellers. It added up to the penny. Your account was credited with that amount. The money was spread around in the cash drawers."

"In other words, there was nothing about it that would enable you to separate it from other currency?"

"Not a thing."

I mopped my forehead. The thing was getting under my skin. I said, "Look, George—you've known me a long time. You know where I work and approximately what I make. Didn't this strike you as odd?"

"Brother, you said it. I telephoned your office. They said you were out of town. So I did the only thing I could do. Legally—or technically—whichever way you want to look at it, the money is yours."

I said, "I didn't write that note, George. I didn't send you the money. It isn't mine, and I don't want it."

"You're stuck with it, just the same."

"What do you mean: I'm stuck with it?"

He explained patiently. "The whole thing was unusual. I had no choice but to follow the directions in that note. It never occurred to me that you hadn't sent it, and it was perfectly good money. The note sounded like you. I certainly couldn't be expected to detect anything wrong about the situation. Lots of queer things happen in any branch of a big bank like ours. I had tried to check with you. No soap. There's no way now of identifying a single one of those bills. If you wanted to draw against it right now, we'd have to honor your check. And that's the picture."

"The more you talk," I said, "the crazier it gets. If somebody wanted to present me with that much money, why did they do it this way?"

"I wouldn't be knowing that. Just as I didn't know whether you'd suddenly hit it rich."

"What do I do now?"

"You can put it in a separate account, if you wish. Or leave it where it is until you find the answer. Meanwhile, one of the ace detectives of the Bankers' Protective Association happens to be with the chief right now. How about telling it to him?"

I nodded. One of the three men walked away, and a few minutes later a man-mountain hove in sight. I was introduced. They said his name was Hanvey. Jim Hanvey.

Hanvey didn't look like a detective. He didn't look like anything except a man who had eaten too much for too long. Large as he was, his clothes were even larger. He had a round face, pink cheeks, sparse hair and a pleasant smile. He had eyes like a fish: gray, dead, sleepy-looking eyes. He took a chair and listened while George Larsen did some explaining. And all the while he fiddled with a gleaming golden gadget that hung suspended from the hawser-like watch chain which spanned his vest. The thing fascinated me until he explained that it was a solid gold toothpick. I decided immediately that I had at last found something I could give my worst enemy for Christmas.

Hanvey was a good listener, although I wasn't sure he was listening. It looked like 6-2-and-even that he was asleep. Larsen finished talking, and then for quite a while there was a lot of silence. Then Hanvey asked, in a slow, drawling, patient voice, "You got no ideas, Mr. Douglas?"

"No. The thing makes a lot of no sense."

"I wish somebody would play a trick like that on me." He gave vent to a tremendous sigh. "I'd buy me a little place in the country and raise chickens."

That didn't seem to call for an answer. He gave me plenty of time, and then he said, "I reckon you want us to look into it for you, huh?"

"Yes."

"You understand that it's your business and you can keep it that way if you want."

"I'd rather lay it in your lap."

"It's a big lap." He chuckled. "Mind if I ask you a few questions?"

"Go ahead."

His questions were simple enough. My name, age, profession, salary, habits, friends. When I finished, he gazed fondly at his golden toothpick and said, "We've missed something somewhere. This thing wasn't accidental. Your name wasn't picked out of a hat. It was somebody who knew you. They knew you had an account here and they probably knew you were out of town, so there couldn't be a quick check-up. You say that note sounds as though you could have written it?"

"Yes. There's not much style to it, but what there is, is mine."

"And you have no rich friends who might like the idea of playing genii to your Aladdin?"

"I haven't any rich friends. And if they wanted to give me that much money, they wouldn't do it that way. What's more: I don't like it."

Hanvey looked me over deliberately. "You're a big guy, Mr. Douglas. You don't look like someone who would scare easy."

"I still don't like something I can't understand."

He asked a shrewd question: "Could you use a hundred thousand?"

"Who couldn't?"

"I don't mean that. I mean, have you got any special iron in the fire? Have you got some scheme on tap which you could put across if you had that much dough?"

"You mean, have I any special use—at this moment—for a large sum of money?"

"Uh-huh."

"No."

"Suppose it was really yours. What would you do with it?"

"Leave it in the bank, I suppose. Buy war bonds. I don't need extra money, if that's what you mean."

Hanvey said, "It's the screwiest thing I've ever run across. Want me to plug on it?"

"If you will."

"Let's let it ride as it is for a while. Mr. Larsen will pass the word around to watch carefully all checks bearing your signature. Though it isn't likely that anybody would try to withdraw that money with a forged check. Meanwhile, just forget that you've got it."

I shook my head. "Fine chance. Could you?"

"Nope. But I could try."

We talked a little more, and then I want back to the office.

21

I chatted with my bosses and, in the course of our conversation, asked them whether they'd made a deposit to my credit while I was away. The senior partner said, "No. Why?"

I tried to pass it off as a joke. I said the bank was crediting me with more money than I had. I didn't say how much. I left the impression that it was a small sum. They both laughed and one of them said something about this being my lucky year. I wasn't so sure he was right.

It was Saturday, and I drifted into a picture show with the idea of forgetting what had happened. I was tired of thinking in circles. But I kept on doing just that. I still don't know what the picture was about. At five o'clock I dropped a nickel in the slot of a pay phone and dialed Dana's number. Her voice gave me the usual thrill. I asked if I could come by her apartment and she said she'd been waiting two hours for just that.

Dana lived in a simple, inexpensive two-room apartment. She had a part-time maid, but she was alone when I got there, which was swell with me. She was wearing a crepe housecoat of black with a broad red stripe down the front. She had on black satin mules, and her toenails had red polish on them. She looked pretty as seventeen dollars' worth of lettuce, and didn't appear to mind my attempts to spoil her lipstick.

Never before had love struck me as so goofy. What a probably excellent picture had failed to do in two hours, Dana accomplished in five minutes. I forgot everything except how lovely she was and how I wished I was married to her. It wasn't until later that I remembered what I had come for.

I sat her down alongside me and told the story. She let me finish without interruption. Then she said, "That's the most ridiculous thing I ever heard."

I agreed with her. She said, "Have you had any fresh ideas since you finished talking with the fat detective?"

"No good ones."

"How about ones that are not so good?"

I said, "Ricardo?" and finished with a rising inflection. Her answer was, "Why?"

I said I couldn't figure why. It was scarcely the act of someone who didn't like another person, but if it was part of a scheme to cause trouble . . .

22

Dana shook her head. "It doesn't come out right anyway, darling. Ricardo hasn't got a dime."

I was puzzled. I knew the act was drawing down fifteen hundred dollars a week. Deducting ten per cent agent's commission, that left $1,350. It was Ricardo's act—his personal property. He paid Dana three hundred dollars a week, and the rest was his, minus income tax. I figured that at a thousand a week gross income, a man could be pretty well heeled.

Dana shook her head. "Gambling," she told me. "He's always believed that he's smarter than the horses. Now that they've shut down all American race tracks, he'll find some other way of losing his money. Maybe by placing bets for the Havana and Mexican tracks. But he'll lose it. He always has, and he always will. Besides, I can't figure any reason why he should put a hundred thousand dollars in your account."

I said, "I can't figure why anyone would. That's what worries me."

We tossed it back and forth and got exactly nowhere. The more we thought about it, the more ridiculous it seemed. She said, "So when we ate steak last night, we weren't pretending. You really *are* worth a lot of money."

"It doesn't make me feel good."

"What will you do about it?"

"Wait. I'm bound to find the answer sooner or later. I can always hope it was a mistake, although I'm sure it wasn't. Whoever it was can have his fortune back any minute he wants it." I leaned forward and my voice tightened up. "But this much I'll promise, my sweet: when I do find the person who did this, I'll also find out why."

She said, "That's a very grim expression you've got on."

"It's the way I feel. The more I think about this, the more I don't like it."

"Meaning what?"

"Not trying to be melodramatic, but it seems to spell trouble."

We both laughed. Which is something we wouldn't have done if we could have looked ahead a few hours.

IV

I took DANA to the Caliente, said I'd be back after the show, and left her. I didn't stay at the club for dinner because this was Saturday night and the room was jammed.

I stopped near the checkroom and bought a pack of cigarettes from a girl named Vivian who wore practically no clothes, as though that would make a man want to smoke. She was a cute little number with lavender eyes, platinum hair and sulky lips. She charged me the usual cabaret excess for the cigarettes but didn't object to accepting the lavish tip which was supposed to make everything all right. She asked me whether I'd been away and I said Yes. She asked how Dana was and I said she was fine. Vivian had a wise look in her young eyes. She had the same ideas about Dana and myself that everybody else had, only she didn't play cute. What we wanted to do was our own business. Only I was getting fed up with folks believing that it was monkey business. No man likes to feel that a decent love is getting muddied up in people's minds.

I stopped near the curb and chatted with Chris, the doorman. We both mentioned that it was cold. We were both right. I figured I might enjoy a walk in the park, but I wasn't quite as hardy as I thought. As I turned the corner the wind hit me. It bit into me like a set of false teeth. I went back to the Caliente. I said, "I'm a softy, Chris. Can't take it."

I went inside and surrendered my hat and coat. A man left his high perch at the bar and I slid into it ahead of another man who missed the chance. I ordered a scotch and plain water. The curtains between the bar and the main dining room were carelessly drawn and I could see the line of cuties doing their stuff. Vivian, the cigarette girl, paused briefly in back of me. She said, "Love is a mess, ain't it, Mr. Douglas?"

The place was full of odors: fish and steak and hors d'œuvres and liquor and powder and perfume. The air was heavy with the smoke of cigarettes and cigars. The music seemed louder than usual, the conversation ditto. I stayed

24

where I was all through the show, getting an occasional glimpse of Dana while her act was on. I called a bus boy, gave him a quarter and asked him to tell Dana where I was. He grinned at me with youthful wisdom and sped off. Twenty minutes later the dance music was on, the guests started crowding the floor and Dana appeared from nowhere. She said, "I'm hungry."

We went out together. Chris commandeered a taxi which arrived at the club with a fresh batch of merrymakers. We gave the address of a little restaurant on the East Side. We had been there a couple of times in the past but we liked it because the food was fair and they had booths where you could talk without cooling the soup on the next table.

We talked about the silly situation at the bank, and about ourselves. We didn't think of any new things to say; the old topics stood up pretty well. A stenographic report of our conversation wouldn't have been listed as literature, but it would have fitted neatly into the love pulps. For two supposedly intelligent people, we could talk sappier than any couple I'd ever met. But then I didn't believe any other couple was ever so much in love.

We didn't kill too much time there. We walked to a newsreel theater and found seats way back in the corner. We took off our gloves and held hands. We sat through a lot of war shots. And laughed like a couple of kids at Donald Duck, who maintained his standing as our favorite actor.

We got back to the club in time for Dana to dress for the 12:30 show. I said I'd wait. I reminded her that the next day was Sunday and I could sleep until noon. Monday morning I'd be a slave again, obeying alarm clocks at seven-thirty. But tonight I was a free agent. She suggested that I come back to her dressing room after the show. Then we could slip out through the next-door tenement under which the dressing rooms were located. That was so she wouldn't be stopped by guests who wanted her to drink with them.

I went back to the bar. This time I wasn't so lucky. Standing room only. I knew what was happening inside by the music. I'd seen that show so many times I knew to the split second who was doing what.

The show dragged. The crowd was high and appreciative.

They encored everything. But it finally ended in a thunder of applause after a second encore by Ricardo & Dana. I shouldered my way between the closely-packed tables, circled the bandstand and turned left in the dreary, drafty corridor. At the far end two doors faced each other. The one on the left was Ricardo's dressing room. The opposite one was Dana's. I rapped and asked, "Are you decent?" which is theatrical vernacular for, "Are you sufficiently dressed?" Dana invited me in.

She had on a robe and was removing her make-up with cold cream. Even that way she looked lovely. Then she went behind a screen to put on her dress. I lighted a cigarette and waited. She came out, looking fresh as a daisy, and asked me where we were going. Before I could answer there came a rap at the door, and Dana said, "Come in."

The man who entered didn't look as though he belonged in the Club Caliente. He was perhaps four inches shorter than I was, and looked hard as a rock. He was dressed in a quiet oxford gray suit, black shoes, gray shirt and dark blue necktie. He had rugged features and a dark complexion. His eyes were bright and black. He removed his hat to disclose the blackest hair I had ever seen. It was close-cropped and neatly brushed.

He looked at Dana and said politely, "Miss Warren?"

"Yes."

Then he looked at me. "Mr. Douglas?"

"Yes."

He smiled. It was a pleasant smile, although rather on the bleak side. He said, "The cigarette girl told me she thought I'd find you in here."

He reached into his pocket and pulled out something. When he turned his hand palm up, we saw what it was. It was the gold badge of a member of the New York City detective force.

"I'm Max Gold," he explained. "Lieutenant Max Gold."

We said we were pleased to meet him, and Dana invited him to have a chair. He sat down stiffly and tried to look friendly. He said, "I hate to intrude. But if I could have a few minutes of your time . . ." He was looking straight at me when he said it.

Dana and I sat down. I said, "You wanted to talk to me?"

"If you don't mind."

"Would it matter if I did?"

He laughed. But there wasn't much mirth in it. He said, "There's something I'd like to ask you about, Mr. Douglas. If you'd rather we were alone . . ."

"Go right ahead. But I know what it's about."

"What?"

"That bank business."

He seemed to be thinking fast and picking his words carefully. "What about it?" he asked.

"I don't know any more than I knew this morning. It made no sense then, and it looks even screwier now."

"In what way?"

"I can't figure it from any angle," I said. "In the first place, I haven't one single friend who owns a hundred thousand dollars. Acquaintances, yes. But friends, no. And if I did, why would they want to give it to me? And if they wanted to give it to me, why would they do it that way?"

"I don't know." He looked down at the toes of his shoes. "Mind going over it again, Mr. Douglas?"

I started at the beginning and went through to the end. I was beginning to feel like a phonograph record. He listened patiently and then nodded.

"Interesting," he commented. "I wish something like that would happen to me."

"You can have my share, lieutenant. Me, I don't like it a little bit. And the very fact that you are here makes me like it less."

"You say you talked with Jim Hanvey this morning?"

"Yes. At the bank. You know him?"

"Sure. He was a captain when I was a patrolman. He's keen."

"He doesn't look it."

"That has fooled a lot of people. He seems to be sleeping half the time. But he doesn't miss a thing. Anyway, that's neither here nor there. I got something else on my mind. Something personal."

I waited. So did he. He didn't seem to be in any hurry.

Finally he raised his sharp, black eyes and asked a direct question.

"How long," he asked, "have you known Ethel Brower?"

I frowned. "Who?"

"Ethel Brower."

I said, "I don't know anybody by that name."

He spoke carefully. "Think hard. Maybe you'll remember."

I tried it. I knew a few women rather well, and a great many casually. Women in the office, telephone girls, girls at the Caliente, wives and sweethearts of friends. I said, "The name doesn't register. What does she do?"

He said, "That's what I'm trying to find out. I think maybe your memory is on vacation. I'm sure you know her."

"Sorry, lieutenant. I'm pretty good on names, and that one simply doesn't click." I was beginning to feel uncomfortable. "Am I supposed to know her?"

"Yeah. Sort of."

Dana had been looking first at him and then at me. She said, "You haven't been holding out on me, have you, Kirk?"

"With something named Ethel Brower? Don't be silly."

Dana turned to Max Gold. "Would she be ravishing, seductive, gorgeous and et cetera? Somebody a man might know and not tell another woman about?"

He smiled back at her. He said, "You and Mr. Douglas are pretty good friends, aren't you, Miss Warren?"

"That's a fair example of understatement."

I said impulsively, "Miss Warren and I are in love with each other. Some day we hope to get married."

Max was still looking at Dana. "You're Ricardo's wife, ain't you?"

"Legally."

"What does that mean?"

"We've been married five years. We lived together for the first six months of that time. Since then we've been nothing more nor less than dance partners."

"But you're still married?"

"Ricardo doesn't like the idea of a divorce."

I broke in. I said, "Look, lieutenant: Didn't you know all this before you came in here?"

He grinned. "I had heard it that way. I didn't know how straight my dope was."

"You knew about Miss Warren and myself, but I have a feeling you didn't know about that bank business."

"That's a good guess, Douglas. I never heard about it until you started talking. But it was interesting—so I listened."

"And so it wasn't what you wanted to see me about, was it?"

"No."

"What *did* you want?"

"We-e-ell . . . first of all I'd like to know what you've been doing all evening."

That puzzled me, but I didn't hesitate. I started with the time I picked up Dana and went right through. When I finished, he turned it over in his mind and then asked quietly, "When you left the club during the dinner show how long were you gone?"

"About five minutes. I spoke to the doorman when I left and also when I came back."

He said, "Cute."

"What does that mean?"

"Why did you speak to him?"

"I always do."

"So he knows you were gone only five minutes?"

"Yes. If he happens to remember." I leaned forward. "What's this all about?"

"I'm just a curious guy. My profession, see? Now about you and Miss Warren: when you went out to dinner together. Does anybody know you in that restaurant?"

"Not by name. Probably not any other way, either—unless the waiter happened to remember."

"And at the picture show: You see anybody there that you knew?"

"No."

"So if somebody didn't want to believe you, you wouldn't have any way of proving you and Miss Warren did just that, would you?"

"Why should I have to prove anything?"

"Keep your shirt on. I was just asking. Cops think that way. Now about this Ethel Brower . . ."

I stood up. I said, "I don't know any such person. I've answered all your questions. Now I'm asking you one. Why I should know a girl named Ethel Brower?"

"I'll tell you." He leaned back in his chair and focused his eyes on my face. Hard. "The reason I figure you ought to know her," he said, "is because she's in your apartment. Right now. And she's dead as hell. She's been murdered."

V

Max gold's keen, black eyes never left my face. If I had anything to give away, he was going to get it. I don't know what he was thinking. I don't know what I was thinking, either.

If he had planned to throw a surprise into me, he had succeeded admirably. I stood there blinking at him, my mouth open and my brain refusing to function. A girl named Ethel Brower—a girl I'd never heard of in my life—dead in my apartment. Murdered. The thing was fantastic. The deposit of one hundred thousand dollars to my account in the bank had been fantastic, too, but not this way.

He waited patiently while I did the conventional things. I moistened my lips. I looked at Dana and she looked at me. I tried to say something and the words stuck. I sat down in a chair. It was his voice which punctured the silence. He said, "I didn't mention it before, but I'm on the homicide squad."

That made everything just dandy. It made me feel fine. If I'd been guilty, I couldn't have felt any guiltier.

He said, smoothly, "You still don't know her?"

"No." The word came out suddenly, like a cork being popped out of a champagne bottle.

"You haven't been to your apartment tonight?"

"No."

"Not even for a few minutes after you finished dinner?"

The answer was still No.

It was Dana who did the first talking for the pair of us.

"He's been with me all evening," she said. "We haven't been near his apartment."

"You and him . . ." Gold's voice was flat. "You're sweethearts. You alibi him and he alibis you. I'd like it to be better than that."

I realized suddenly that Dana was caught right in the middle of this mess. I said, "Look, lieutenant: She wasn't anywhere near that apartment. She doesn't know anything about it."

"About what?"

"This girl; this Ethel Brower."

He said to Dana, "You never heard of her, either?"

"No."

"Doesn't it strike you as queer she'd pick the apartment of a perfect stranger to get murdered in?"

I made an effort to pull myself together. I'm a big boy, and I can look after myself under ordinary circumstances. But I had been thoroughly shaken by this cold, impersonal man with the piercing eyes and the curly black hair.

I said, "Would you mind telling me what happened? And how you heard about it?"

He thought that one over. He said, "Your apartment house is pretty big, Douglas. Have you ever left an order that the package-room could put things inside if you weren't there?"

"Yes."

"Well, that's how they found out. The boy from the grocery store delivered some stuff for you. You weren't there. He took it to the package-room. The package-room boy telephoned your apartment. No answer. He told the night superintendent. They went up together. They went in. The place was dark, so they switched on the ceiling light. They seen this girl—this Ethel Brower—in that gray chair you got near the reading light. She was fast asleep. Only she looked kind of funny. The super took another look. He seen right away that she was dead as a mackerel. It wasn't until after he reported it and our medical examiner got there that we found out how she died. She'd been strangled. And I suppose you're still surprised, aren't you?"

Dana reached over and took my hand. I said to the detective, "Are you arresting me?"

"Nope. Not now, anyway. I'll come clean. We ain't got a thing on you except it happened in your apartment. We wouldn't want you to be going off on another trip right away, but we don't like to arrest anybody if we can't make it stick."

I said, "Thanks." And I meant it. This was my first experience with New York policemen; and if Max Gold was a sample, I liked 'em. He was a hard, efficient man doing a job.

He said, "I'd like you to go over there with me, Douglas. You too, Miss Warren, if you don't mind."

"I don't mind." Dana stood up before I could argue against it. She smiled at me. "I know it won't be pleasant, Kirk. But I think the lieutenant wants me . . ."

"Yes, Miss. Maybe you might recognize her. She ain't bad to look at. Sort of asleep-looking, like I said. At first we thought maybe it was a natural death."

"You're sure it wasn't?"

"We're sure."

I said, "But if she was strangled there must be fingerprints on her throat. They would prove . . ."

"Sorry. It doesn't work out that way. We get fingerprint traces off a dead body, but there ain't enough characteristics left to identify 'em. It's something we ain't solved yet. But the minute somebody dies, the fingerprints on the flesh ain't any better than if they wasn't left there in the first place." He got up, put his hat on. "If you'll come along with me . . ."

There was a car parked a short distance down the street from the club. It was a plain black sedan. Lieutenant Gold held open the door, then joined us in the back. To the driver he said, "On your way, Joe. Back to the apartment."

Dana and I huddled together. We didn't say anything, but I knew she was thinking as hard as I was, which was plenty hard.

Too much was happening too fast. There were too many questions and too few answers. The hundred thousand dollars in my name at the bank commenced to frighten me. I believed that it was connected with the dead girl in my apartment. It couldn't be coincidence. I said, "Whoever it was: I wonder why they picked on me."

"Yeah." That was Max Gold speaking. "I been kinda wondering that, too."

Only once more did he speak during our trip to the West Side. He addressed Dana. "On account it's murder," he said, "I got to ask personal questions: Even if you ain't living with your husband, wouldn't you figure him to get sore if he thought you were playing around with Mr. Douglas here?"

She shook her head. "I don't mean a thing to Ricardo. I'm just his dance partner. He knows all about Kirk and me."

Max said thoughtfully, "But with a name like that. You know, hot Latin blood . . ."

"He was born and raised in Brooklyn."

"I thought that was a gag."

"It's the truth."

"Then the name is a phoney?"

"No. His father was Puerto Rican."

"Then we could say his blood might be half hot, huh?" Max chuckled dryly. "He could maybe of been madder than you think. He could maybe of seen this dame going to Douglas's apartment and followed her in, thinking it was you . . ."

I said sharply, "That's ridiculous. If he'd been that kind of a person, he'd have done something long ago. Besides, you can't strangle a woman without knowing who she is—or isn't. And what's more, you don't believe it yourself."

"I didn't say I did. Me, I just try to find out."

We reached the apartment house. There were no police cars, no policemen. The doorman looked at me peculiarly and the elevator man was obviously in on the know. The hallway was empty. It was all very tranquil.

I unlocked the door and let them in. A huge man blocked our entrance. Then he recognized Max Gold and said, "Hi, lieutenant."

Gold nodded. "Any telephone calls since I been gone?"

"No."

"Fingerprint boys and D.A. men all finished?"

"Long ago."

"Okay . . ." Gold led the way. Dana and I followed, pressing each other's hands.

The room looked just as it had when I'd left, except that on the floor near the kitchenette was a box of groceries. Just a box of groceries and a very ordinary-looking girl asleep in the chair by the reading light. I didn't have to look twice to realize that she wasn't ever going to wake up.

Max Gold stood against the wall. He was watching Dana and me. So was the man who had been guarding the apartment.

I stared at the dead girl. My guess at her age would have been the very early thirties. She was about Dana's height. She was thin. She had dark hair. I couldn't tell what color her eyes were because they were closed. I couldn't see any signs of violence or any bruises on her throat.

She was wearing a black cloth coat with a heavy fur collar which could have been fox or skunk. It was open, and I could see the dark brown dress underneath. She had on a brown hat. Her legs were encased in sheer stockings which looked like nylon, and her feet were swallowed up by galoshes. She wasn't pretty and she wasn't homely. She looked like the sort of girl you could see a hundred times and never remember. I tried my best to place her and met with no luck. I turned to Max Gold and said, "As far as I can remember, I never saw her before in my life."

Dana said, "Neither did I."

Max sighed. "The night super never saw her before, either. Nor the package-room boy. Nor the doorman. Nobody knows her. Or why she came here. Especially me."

I asked, "How did you know her name?"

"The bag. We went through it. Social security card. A credit tag from a department store. A letter from some girl friend in Moline. It didn't tell us a thing except her name and address. But we'd still like to know what she was doing here." He stared at me. "And I also been wondering how she got in."

I said, "So have I."

Max sighed. "I guess we'll cart her off to the morgue." He said something to the big plainclothesman and that gentleman started telephoning. I said, "What happens now?"

"About what?"

"Me."

"Nothing. You ain't under arrest, if that's what you're asking. There'll be an inquest. The District Attorney's office will probably talk to you. Maybe that'll lead to the Grand Jury.

It usually doesn't unless the D.A. thinks he's got something solid to work on."

"Then I'm not under suspicion?"

"Sure you are. You and Miss Warren both. You gotta be. That doesn't mean I think you did it. But I can't get it out of my mind that you're both mixed up in it."

"Will it be in the newspapers?"

He nodded. "That's another thing that can't be avoided. Also, it might help. Publicity sometimes uncovers a lot of angles we couldn't find. But for the present Miss Warren will be kept out of it. It ain't her apartment, and even though the boys are probably lousy with her fingerprints we won't pay too much attention to that, because you admit that she drops in here lots."

I thanked him. He was being damned decent. I went into the kitchen, poured a drink of brandy. Dana said No when I offered it, so I made her swallow it. Gold and the other cop compromised for a bottle of beer each.

We didn't do much talking while we waited for the morgue wagon. I turned Dana's chair around and did the same with mine, so we wouldn't have to stare at Ethel Brower.

They finally took her away. Max told us good night. He suggested I let him know if I ran across anything. I didn't know what he was thinking, and I wasn't so sure I wanted to know.

For all his cordiality, for all my innocence: I was afraid.

The way I looked at it, he couldn't help thinking that I had killed Ethel Brower. He was digging patiently for evidence to use against me. All I had was breathing time.

That seemed to check it up to me. I sat down. Dana came and sat on my lap. She put her arms around me. She started to cry.

VI

I LOOKED AT the little white clock on the mantel. It showed five minutes before three. Outside, everything was quiet except for the occasional sound of taxi tires on hard-packed

35

snow. My apartment looked about as usual: everything just so, everything neat. No cops, no Ethel Brower, no anything to indicate that a murder had been committed.

Dana's slim body was shaking. Her arms were tight. She had held up magnificently while the pressure was on but now that the first act was over, reaction hit her.

I let her cry. I knew it would do her good. I just sat there holding her close. My left arm was around her. With my right hand I patted her shoulder and made reassuring sounds. It would have sounded silly if it hadn't been so serious.

After a while she stopped crying. Then she got up, crossed to the gateleg table where she had left her bag, and took out compact and lipstick. I just watched her, letting her handle things her own way.

She dabbed at her face with the cosmetics. Her eyes and the corners of her mouth showed evidence of the strain to which she had been subjected. She finished what she was doing and walked toward me. She said, "I'm all right now."

I got up and poured two brandies. She drank hers and I swallowed mine in a gulp. It burned all the way down and took away some of the chill inside me. But it didn't make me feel any better, or any less bewildered.

I reached for my pipe and tamped tobacco in the bowl. She took a cigarette. I lighted it for her, then started my pipe going. She said, "You really haven't any idea who she was, Kirk?"

"No, dear."

She picked her words carefully. "If you did—you'd tell me?"

"Yes."

"You wouldn't be afraid that I'd be jealous?"

"No."

We sat staring at each other. Dana said, "This . . . and the bank. They must be connected some way."

"They must be."

I puffed harder and thought harder. I said, "There's somewhere I want to go. Right now. I'd like you to come along if you think you can take it."

She repeated, "I'm all right." Then she added, "Where?"

"Just a few blocks. The McKinley Hospital. I want to talk to Arthur."

"Arthur . . . ?" Then she got the idea and nodded. She knew I was referring to one of my few close friends in New York. Dr. Arthur Maybank, five months an M.D. and now serving a nine-months' interneship. She said, "Didn't he stay here while you were away, Kirk?"

"Yes. You don't know what it means to an interne to have a place outside the hospital on his off nights."

She glanced at the chair in which the body of Ethel Brower had been sitting. "You think maybe Arthur knew her?"

"It's possible. I want to find out."

"Why didn't you tell the police?"

"I didn't want to get him mixed up in it. He's never had anything but bad breaks since he was a kid. Why should I throw him into the middle of this unless he knew the girl?"

"Will he be frank with you?"

I shrugged. "It doesn't matter. I've known him a long time. I'll be able to tell."

On our way out we were stared at again by the elevator operator and the doorman. I could see that they were busting with curiosity and would have given a pretty to ask a few questions. Dana and I walked to the hospital.

The McKinley was a block wide and half of an avenue-block in length. It was an ancient graystone building which once had been New York's leading hospital. Now it was old and worn out. There had been talk of tearing it down and rebuilding on the same site, but the war had postponed those plans.

There was an old-fashioned iron fence along the front. Two gateways had been cut through it, one for doctors' automobiles and the other for ambulances. There was a white sign with unkempt black letters which read "Accident Entrance" and an arrow pointing to a double door under a porte-cochère. I said, "Arthur told me he was on accident for three months. If he's around, we'll find him here."

We walked inside. There was a narrow little entrance and a pint-size reception room. A girl sat on a hard wooden bench reading a confession magazine. She wore thick-lensed glasses. At first she paid no attention to us and I thought she must

37

be the friend of a patient. She looked up without interest. "You a doctor?" she asked. I said No, half expecting her to inquire what the hell I was doing there but she didn't. She had asked her question, got her answer, and was no longer interested. Dana and I rambled around.

To the right of the reception room was a plate-glass window which was the front of a cubicle of an office. A languid young lady sat inside gazing at a typewriter. There was a piece of paper under the platen, but she wasn't doing anything about it. Nor about us, either.

We went through a doorway and stepped into a big square room. There were four or five surgical wagons standing around forlornly. There was an enameled instrument case with a lot of the enamel chipped off so that it showed black splotches. At the far side of that room was another door through which I could see a double bank of green steel lockers. A man in a blue uniform and a big blond youth in white were smoking and talking. Nobody paid any attention to us.

We went back to the reception room, and I managed to attract the attention of the girl who was doing nothing about the typewriter. I said, "I'd like to speak to Dr. Arthur Maybank."

She looked at me with blank eyes. Then she said in a bored voice, "He ain't on duty."

"Is he in?"

"If he is, he's sleeping."

"I'm a friend of his. I wish you'd give him a ring."

"He ain't on duty," she said, and that's all she did say. She started poking at the typewriter keys. I took Dana's arm and we went outside again. We walked down the block and re-entered the building through the main entrance.

This was larger than the accident room and not quite as dirty. There still wasn't any rousing welcome. A worried, middle-aged woman sat in another chair, holding a sleepy little girl. There was another glassed-in cage in which I saw another bored young woman and a switchboard. I walked over and repeated my request for Dr. Arthur Maybank.

The girl put up an argument. She said Dr. Maybank was asleep and that it was against the rules to disturb him. I worked on her. She finally plugged in, waited a long while—

about as long as it would take to wake someone from a sound sleep—and then started talking. She told Arthur that a man and a woman were downstairs to see him and that she hadn't been able to brush them off. I told her to say that it was Kirk Douglas and Dana Warren and that it was important. She said it, then snapped the plug out and looked at us. She said, "He's coming now," and promptly lost all interest in us.

Dana said, "What a depressing place. I don't wonder Arthur would want to use your apartment on his off nights."

An ancient elevator stopped on the lobby floor. The door clanked open and Arthur Maybank stepped out. His eyes looked heavy with sleep. He had pulled trousers and a coat over his pajamas. His feet were encased in bedroom slippers.

Arthur never was an inspiring figure, but in this costume he was even less so. He was small and looked even smaller than his 135 pounds. His hair was sparse and old-looking in spite of the fact that he was only twenty-six. His coloring was mousy. He looked like a young man who had been slapped around by life. He certainly didn't look like a Lothario.

I had known him for years. We were close without being intimate. He had scraped and struggled and sweated to get through college and medical school. He was serving his interneship without pay. They all do but most of them have a little income. Arthur didn't. He was grateful as a pup for small favors, and I had let him use my apartment while I was away because I knew that it looked like a palace to him. It was because he had been buffeted so much that I had hesitated to drag him into the case.

He seemed surprised to see us. He shook hands with us, and smiled at Dana. She smiled right back, though I knew she wasn't feeling much like smiling.

I apologized for waking him. He said that was all right. Whatever you did to Arthur was always all right. I said, "Can we sit down somewhere?"

We went to a corner of the lobby. We arranged three stiff wooden chairs in a little circle. I said, "I want to ask you something, Arthur. If the answer is Yes, it's okay by me. But I want you to come clean."

He nodded. "You know I will."

39

"Sure I know." I cast around for the right way of starting. "While I was away you used my apartment, didn't you?"

"Sure. On my off nights. You don't know how good it feels to get away from this joint."

"I can imagine. What did you do in the apartment?"

He frowned. "Slept. And read. And just sat there figuring how lucky I was to get a break like that."

"What else?"

"You'll laugh. I fixed my own dinners. I'm a lousy cook, but they tasted wonderful. I even enjoyed washing the dishes. Then I'd sit in the corner and read and hope that some day I'd be successful enough to afford an apartment like that."

I said, "Did you do any helling around?"

"Any *what?*"

"Any stepping? Briefly, did you entertain any girl friends?"

"I haven't any girl friends," he said simply.

I started over. "I'm driving at something. On the level, it's fine with me if you did. I just wanted to know."

He shook his head. "Even if I'd known any girls who would have liked to come up there, Kirk—I wouldn't have done it."

"Why?"

"Because . . . well, it wouldn't have seemed right."

"You aren't embarrassed because Dana is listening, are you?"

They exchanged smiles. "I can take Dana in stride," he said. "As a matter of fact, if I had been partying I'd probably boast about it." A worried frown appeared on his forehead. He said, "Did you find something broken—or missing? Is that it?"

"No. But before I explain, I've got one more question. Did you ever hear of—a girl named Ethel Brower?"

I could see him thinking. Then he shook his head. "No, Kirk. Not that I remember. I meet lots of people here at the hospital. But if you mean it's somebody I should remember . . . I don't."

"Did any girl show up at the apartment at any time you were there? Anybody asking for me, perhaps?"

"I never saw a soul." He looked concerned. "I wish you'd explain all this, Kirk. You and Dana wouldn't be here if it wasn't important."

40

I told him the story of Ethel Brower. When I finished, he said, "My God! And you thought maybe she was someone I'd been playing around with?"

"No, I didn't. But I knew I didn't know her, and I figured that if she'd been a guest of yours there, and if she had perhaps thought it was your apartment and had come back to see you . . ."

He seemed shocked. He said, "Is she still there?"

"No. They carried her to the morgue."

"Would you like me to go over and take a look?"

"Better stay out of it, Arthur."

He turned to Dana. "He should have told them about me."

"Why?" she asked. "There wasn't any sense dragging you in unless it turned out that you had known the girl."

He said, "Gee! you're a thoughtful pair." He looked small and helpless. "Is there something I can do?"

"Yes. First, go back to bed. Second, forget the whole thing."

"And," finished Dana, "forgive us for waking you."

We practically shoved him into the elevator and sent him back to his room. We stepped into the bitter cold of black morning. I said, "One block away there's a diner. It'll be warm there, and the coffee will be hot. Let's go."

The diner was hot all right. There was a long counter with stools in front of it. Behind the counter was a man in a greasy apron. He was tossing some hamburgers for a couple of truckmen. Onions were sizzling on the griddle.

I ordered two hamburgers and two black coffees. We were served and Dana started eating. So did I.

She said, "I wonder whether the police have talked to Ricardo."

Ricardo!

We looked at each other. We didn't say anything. But the name "Ricardo" was hanging between us in the steamy air.

VII

W HEN I tumbled into bed, the little white clock told me it was half past five. I didn't feel sleepy but I hoped I was, because I didn't want to lie there thinking. I've got good muscles and fair nerves, but murdered ladies were new to me, and being the subject of police investigation was new, too.

I was lucky. I went to sleep. The next thing I knew two taxi drivers were arguing like crazy in front of the apartment house entrance, and it was ten minutes before noon. I got up, closed the windows, turned on the heat, put some coffee in the percolator, drank some orange juice, and climbed back into bed to wait for the apartment to warm up.

The warming-up process took about the same length of time as the coffee. I got up again, poured myself a cup of it, took two scalding sips, lighted a cigarette, and then went to the door and picked up the Sunday paper. I looked at the big headlines on the first page. There was nothing about me or Ethel Brower. That was inside, on page six.

And even on page six there wasn't much. It seemed that a very unimportant lady had expired in the apartment of an even more unimportant man. Probably murder. The article gave my name, age, former army service and profession. It stated that the police were following leads and that I wasn't under arrest. Max Gold had given out the story nicely. It didn't read dirty. Apparently the young lady had dropped in for a social call on a perfect stranger and had been strangled. It didn't make sense, but then I couldn't figure it, either.

Halfway through my second cup of coffee the buzzer sounded and I opened the door for Lieutenant Max Gold. He gave me a cordial good morning, nodded to my invitation to join me in a cup of coffee, and then said, "How's tricks this morning, Douglas?"

"I don't know. I just finished reading about myself. It was decent of you to hand it to the reporters that way."

"I aim to please." He smiled. "Any hunches?"

"No."

"Still can't remember the dame?"

"No. But I feel certain that I never met her, even casually."

He said, "What I'm here for: Maybe you were playing cute last night on account Miss Warren was along. Maybe you do have some fun on the side."

"Try again, lieutenant."

He sighed. "I wasn't sold on it myself. But sometimes a man will take chances on covering up rather than let his girl know he'd stray." He glanced around the apartment. He said, "I been checking on Ethel Brower. She doesn't add up to be the kind of girl anybody would want to murder. Of course we haven't finished, but I think we got the essential dope."

I still didn't say anything. Gold went on:

"The house where she was living is a nice, respectable, quiet place in the Eighties between West End Avenue and Riverside. Cost her $90 a month. Furnishings to match. Adding everything up, I figure it cost her about $250 a month to live. That ain't dough, but it ain't hay, neither. She's been there a couple of years. Had so few visitors the doorman and elevator ops can't peg any one in particular. Personal effects don't tell us a thing. Check book didn't tell us anything, either. Balance seemed to stick between $500. and $1,000. Lived alone. Didn't work. Maybe she had a small income, and maybe somebody was laying it on the line for her. I'll know more tomorrow when I get a report from her bank . . . whether her deposits were by cash or check. So far she comes out zero. The stuff we got at her apartment looks just the same as she did."

"And there's nothing more to tie me up with her?"

"Nope. We dusted for prints. Yours weren't among those present."

"Why are you telling me all this?"

"So you'll get the idea we're playing on the same team. Let's say you didn't kill her. Let's even admit you didn't know her. You just the same rock along for a lot of years and nothing happens to you. Then all of a sudden somebody slaps a hundred grand in the bank for you—and they do it smooth. A girl drifts up here and gets knocked off in your best chair. It could be you'd try to help us to help you."

I said, "I wish I could. I'm more than a little apprehensive."

"You don't look like a guy who would scare easy."

"You'd be surprised."

"What you scared about?"

"If I knew, I wouldn't be scared. I just have a feeling that I haven't heard the last of this."

"You got something there, buddy. If you're leveling with me somebody has chosen you to play patsy. Meanwhile, if anything comes along, telephone me. Homicide Bureau. And if I'm not there, call Centre Street and ask 'em to find me." He got up and put on his hat. "You'll have reporters in your hair. You can tell them just what you've told me. Except maybe it would be better not to mention the bank angle. Also there'll be an inquest. You can leave out the bank story there, too. But tell the rest of it like you say it happened." He grinned at me and put his hand on the doorknob. But he didn't turn it. As though as an afterthought, he said "You and this lad Ricardo ever tangle?"

I shook my head.

"Him and Miss Warren don't play house?"

"No. You can check on that."

"I did already." The smile he gave me was warm. "But if I was Ricardo and was married to a classy chick like that, I wouldn't like having another guy trespassing."

He went out. It was his opinion and he was entitled to it. I sat down and started wondering whether I'd figured Ricardo wrong. I knew how Dana felt about him, but how could I be certain as to what he felt about her. It was a new idea and not very reassuring.

During the early afternoon a couple of reporters showed up. I followed Max Gold's advice, and didn't mention the bank. I didn't mention Dana, either. The reporters seemed only mildly interested. They made it clear that the only reason they bothered with it at all was because there wasn't any logical explanation of how the girl got into my place and who killed her. They listened to what I had to say, looked the place over, and confined their comments to "Whaddaya know about that?" and "It's screwy as hell, isn't it?"

Waiting for the phone call which I knew would come in

44

sooner or later from Dana, I went over to my drawing board and tried to concentrate on some work. Nothing doing. I knew I'd be all right in the office when the work was laid out for me, but this little extra stuff I'd been doing at home had lost its savor. I was glad when Dana called about three o'clock; I was glad to taxi over to her place; I was glad to get my arms around her.

We did a lot of talking, but couldn't cook up a single new idea. Finally, we agreed that we'd discard the whole thing unless a fresh thought came along.

At 7:30 I took her to the club. We sat at my pet corner table near the corridor and took our time. We didn't start eating until after the dinner show. Ricardo changed from tails to street clothes and paused at our table. He said, "Nice publicity you got this morning, Douglas."

I looked at him and nodded.

He said, "I didn't know you were a chaser." He smiled under his thin moustache. "Though I should have, seeing that you and my wife have been playing around so long."

That was supposed to infuriate me, and it did, but I tried not to let him see it. He went on, "A cop has been talking to me. Fellow named Gold. He was asking about you and Dana."

"What did you tell him?"

"I gave it to him the way I see it. It would have been fun to play the outraged husband, but I figured it wouldn't get over. Then he wanted to know where I was last night."

"What did you tell him?"

"Nothing very impressive. I was at a movie—just like you said you were. He didn't think that was much of an alibi."

He waited for me to say something. He was disappointed. I had a headful of ideas but that's all they were. After a while Ricardo moved away. "Have fun at the inquest," he said.

I turned in before midnight and slept soundly. At the office Monday morning the boys started firing questions at me. I played it Max Gold's way. The big bosses called me in and asked me about it. I told my story and they seemed to believe most of what I said. I felt foolish and impotent, and I couldn't escape the conclusion that they couldn't quite swallow the idea that I'd never even know the Brower woman.

45

The inquest was undramatic and astonishingly brief. They asked me a lot of routine questions. The verdict was that Ethel Brower came to her death at the hands of a person, or persons, unknown.

I ate alone, had a telephone conversation with Dana, grabbed another long night's sleep, and by Tuesday the newspapers and the rest of the world appeared to have forgotten me and my troubles. That evening, after leaving the office, I went to the Caliente to wait for Dana. I got there at eight o'clock, said a brief hello, and sat at my usual corner table.

Dana came back long before time for her act. She was dressed to go on and she looked like a million dollars. We talked about where we'd eat later, and while we were discussing it there was a commotion near the entrance. The paying guests quit looking at the lovelies on the floor, and every eye in the place was focused on the party of four which swept in and accepted a ringside table from a head waiter.

There were three men and one woman in the group, and it didn't require any Sherlock Holmes instinct to grab the idea that it was the girl who was getting the attention.

She was tall and statuesque. She had lots of curves and had them in the right places. The dress, which she wore under an ermine wrap, wasn't calculated to leave you guessing.

She had honey-blonde hair and eyes so deeply blue that they looked like sapphires. Her skin was clear and very blonde. Her hair-do was the formal kind with a lot of set waves and tight little curls. There was one curl falling over her forehead, but I had a hunch that even this little detail was studied; that it represented a conscious effort to look careless.

Her three escorts waited for her to remove the ermine wrap. She took her time about it. She knew that people were staring. She loved it. I didn't know who she was, but I'd been around enough to realize that she must be something extra special.

She was lovely, if you like that sort of loveliness. Smooth and confident. Her lips were full and sensual. Her bored smile was rehearsed. She couldn't have been more than twenty-two.

I glanced at Dana. Her eyes were sparkling and she was shaking her head as though she couldn't believe it.

Scarcely had the young lady seated herself when two photographers appeared. Nobody paid any attention to the show. Flash bulbs popped. And a waiter, passing our table en route to the kitchen, said aloud, "I'll be damned! It's her all right."

I said to Dana, "What is it?"

She looked at me incredulously. You don't know?"

"I do not. And apparently I'm the only ignorant person here."

"That," she said, "is twenty million dollars!"

"Has it got a name?"

"I'll say." She smiled at me. "You poor, unsophisticated man. That is Candy Livingston."

I promptly joined the Starers Club. "Candy Livingston!" I echoed. "Twenty million bucks and a chassis like that!"

Dana said, "The papers have been full of her recently. But maybe not where you've been."

"Even there they didn't exactly ignore her," I said. "Hasn't she recently returned from being kidnaped?"

"About ten days ago. They paid a half million dollars' ransom."

"Could be," I commented. "Who paid it?"

"She did. She'll never miss it. But what surprises me is how soon she's stepped into circulation again."

I said, "She doesn't look like the shrinking violet type."

"She isn't. But this has been a different sort of publicity."

"Tell me about it. I'm quivering with eagerness."

"It's quite a story," Dana explained. "She disappeared in November, except that nobody knew she had disappeared."

"Not very logical."

"With her it is. That twenty million is hers. Various forbears dug it out of the Pennsylvania earth. They dug it, cashed it in, and died. I understand that Candy has been sampling life pretty liberally since she was seventeen." Then Dana laughed and added, "Believe it or not, her name is Clara."

"Doesn't fit. Nothing like that could be named Clara."

"That's why the columnists changed it. They discovered a

47

childhood nickname and tied it on her. More glamour to it. And easier to remember."

"She'd be hard to forget," I said. "In fact, she looks like a young lady who doesn't want to be forgotten. Who kidnaped her?"

"Nobody knows. She swears even she doesn't. Anyway, when she vanished, nobody knew it was a kidnaping. She was always pulling stunts like that. She'd go away and neglect to let her friends know. Nobody suspected she'd been kidnaped until she telephoned her lawyers to get together a half million dollars in cash. She insisted that the police and the F. B. I. were to be left out of it. The lawyers paid the money to a man who met them in Central Park near Fifth Avenue. The next day Candy came home. That was a week ago last Friday, the twenty-sixth. It was the day after the worst blizzard New York had in twenty years. The Saturday papers carried the story."

Dana's attitude amused me. "What fascinates you so?" I asked. "The twenty million, the kidnaping, or the lady herself?"

"All three. But mostly, the girl. I met her once at some club. She wouldn't remember. But I was amazed. She's nice. A little crude, perhaps. A little boisterous . . . but regular."

I said, "You intrigue me. If I weren't a rich man myself, I'd make a play."

Ricardo loomed over us. He was too interested to be unpleasant. He asked, "Isn't that Candy Livingston?"

Dana said, "Yes."

He stated that he'd be damned, which was just what I had heard a waiter say. Obviously, Miss Livingston was creating all the excitement she could have desired.

The emcee was announcing Ricardo & Dana. Ricardo went to the other side of the bandstand. Dana stood up and waited. Then they were on the floor, and once again I was in this world and Dana in another. Once again I punished myself by watching her dance. For these few minutes she was always lost to me.

But even the artistry of Ricardo & Dana couldn't hold the attention of the crowd tonight. It was Candy Livingston. There was only polite applause at the end of the act, not enough to justify an encore. Dana came back to my table. Ricardo was with her. The head waiter joined us, looking excited.

"Mr. Ricardo?" he said. "Miss Dana?"

Ricardo asked him what he wanted.

"It is both of you. Miss Livingston asked whether you will join her table for a drink."

Ricardo didn't hesitate. But Dana delighted me by looking disappointed. She said, "Must I?"

The head waiter nodded. "I am sure the management would appreciate it, Miss Dana."

She glanced at me and made a gesture of unhappiness. She said, "What one must sacrifice for one's art."

"Go ahead," I said. "Later you can tell me how it feels to rub elbows with twenty million dollars. Meanwhile, I'll sit here and sulk."

I watched them cross the floor with the head waiter. Ricardo was excited. He would be. I got a screwball hunch. I thought, "Suppose this Livingston female could fall for Ricardo. He'd love twenty million dollars better than his dance act. Then he'd divorce Dana and I could marry her and we'd name our first girl baby Candy." It was a nice idea, though I couldn't feel positive sure certain that it would work out that way.

The three men at Candy's table stood up. They were nice young fellows who didn't mean a thing. Most likely when the columnists reported on the morrow that Candy Livingston was again on display, they'd forget to mention the names of the three young men . . . and hearts would be broken. The thought made me very sad.

The head waiter was performing the introductions. Candy held out her hand to Dana. She smiled. She had a nice smile. She looked like a girl you might enjoy meeting even if she were only half as rich. Another table was shoved up against theirs and additional chairs were brought. The manager fluttered about the doorway, looking pleased. Then he disappeared, and my guess was that he was telephoning the newspapers. Hot stuff! "The gorgeous Candy Livingston, ex-kidnapee, had herself a time in the Club Caliente last night."

49

I ordered myself a daiquiri and lighted a cigarette. I took out a pencil and doodled on the tablecloth. It wasn't beautiful and it wasn't art. I didn't know anyone had stopped at my table until a voice came down over my shoulder.

It was a full, husky voice, definitely on the pleasant side, and it said, "Lonely, Big Boy?"

I looked up into the deep blue eyes of Candy Livingston. I clambered to my feet. She said, "I'm Candy Livingston."

"I'm Kirk Douglas."

She smiled. "You were included in the invitation. Come along."

I shook my head. "Thanks just the same, Miss Livingston, but . . ."

"No use." Her eyes crinkled at the corners. They were nice eyes. "We need another extra man at my table."

I asked, "Who wished this on you?"

"Miss Warren. She said I fascinated you."

"She was right." So Dana was having fun at my expense, was she? I could handle that. "I think you're terrific," I said. "But I have my pride. I need to be coaxed."

"Pretty please."

I said, "You've got yourself another man, Miss Livingston."

VIII

CANDY LED me to her table and introduced me around. Her three young men popped up out of their seats and announced that they were delighted to meet me. Candy motioned me to a chair next to her. She lifted an eyebrow which was all she had to do to summon a waiter, they were that close.

"Drink?" she asked.

"No, thanks. One more and I'd fall on my face. I haven't eaten."

She ordered three menus and gave one to Dana, Ricardo and me. I protested feebly, but she insisted. She said we'd be there a long time and she didn't like to watch people starving to death.

Dana glanced at me as much as to say, "We're stuck with
50

it," and ordered a club sandwich. That sounded like an excellent compromise, so I said I'd take the same. Ricardo followed suit. We all ordered coffee.

Chatter hung over the table like a fog while things happened in the kitchen. When the three club sandwiches appeared, they weren't sandwiches at all, but productions. Each one looked like a six-course dinner with trimmings. Candy Livingston Specials. The sort of sandwiches you can buy for twenty million dollars.

I was getting a big kick out of this. It was the first time I'd ever been stared at by the mob. Of course I knew that they weren't staring at me but at Candy . . . but I was sitting next to her, and they couldn't miss me, either. I was too honest with myself to pretend that it wasn't fun.

Candy kept a light conversation going while we massacred our sandwiches and drank our coffee. She talked mostly with Dana, and at the same time Ricardo was turning the full force of his Brooklyn-Latin personality on her. I had a hunch that he was thinking precisely what I most wanted him to think; namely, that a ravishing blonde and twenty million dollars were worth a lot of effort.

Candy was cordial enough, but she didn't appear to be impressed. That surprised me because Ricardo was the sort of man that Candy's sort of woman would naturally go for. He was big and handsome and not so refined that it hurt. When the waiter had removed the remains of our scanty meal, Candy asked me to dance with her. I said, "Give yourself a thrill, Miss Livingston. Ricardo is the lad who can dance."

She smiled and said, "I'll take him on later." She got up and held out her hand. There wasn't anything for me to do but follow.

We moved out onto the crowded dance floor. We had plenty of room. I tried to be nonchalant, but it wasn't easy. I felt like something in a zoo.

We got halfway around the floor. I danced just well enough to know that she was really good. She was using some sort of exotic perfume. It was unusual and exciting. I said, "You love being in the spotlight, don't you?"

She bestowed a lingering look on me. It was supposed to

51

burn, and maybe it did—a little. Then she smiled, and I decided for the second time that it was a nice smile.

As a matter of fact, I was reaching the conclusion that Candy was a nice girl. She was too important and too wealthy to be affected. She was what she was, and you could take or leave her alone.

She was slightly less than impersonal in her dancing. The body that was pressed close against mine was a very nice body, and there was lots of it. I got the idea that I was getting the business. I was supposed to roll over and wave my paws in the air.

People were still staring. I could imagine the conjecture, "Who's the big guy with the pushed-in face dancing with Candy Livingston?" That would be me. And the flattened nose wasn't my fault. That was a souvenir from an intercollegiate boxing tournament. The night I forgot to duck. This was another night I wasn't ducking, either.

One of the young men from Candy's retinue was moving around the dance floor with Dana. He swung her close to us and my eye met hers. She looked very much amused, and gave me a broad wink. I tightened my arms around Candy's body, but I was thinking of Dana. Life is like that—sometimes.

Candy looked up at me. She said, "Am I dancing close enough?"

I relaxed my pressure, but she didn't take advantage of the opportunity. I said, "Sorry!" and she said, "Be yourself, Mister. I like it."

I tried to cook up a scintillating retort, but I was fresh out of bright comments. I was also very warm. Miss Livingston's dancing was definitely on the torrid side. It didn't mean a thing, but it would have burnt a hole in an iceberg.

She said abruptly, "What's the verdict?"

"Verdict?" I didn't know what she meant, and probably sounded like a dope.

"Am I what you expected?"

"You're a very nice person."

"How cute! How refined! But not enough."

I said, "I think I'm being taken for a ride. Why trouble yourself?"

She said, "I like you. I'm throwing myself at you. I'd like this to be the beginning of a beautiful friendship."

I laughed and asked, "Why?"

"You want diagrams?" I'll never believe you're that stupid."

"You'd be surprised," I said. "Even my mother never thought I was right bright."

Dana danced near us again. I fancied I detected a faint symptom of displeasure. My ego jumped ten points. For the first time in all the weeks I'd been coming to the Club Caliente, I felt like something more than The-Little-Man-Who-Sits-in-the-Corner.

Candy said a few nice things. At least, I thought they were nice. She said them in a low, husky, intimate voice. The lady was working on me. I started asking myself why.

It wasn't my manly beauty, because I haven't any. It wasn't my sparkling conversation, because I don't sparkle. I had the odd feeling that this whole thing had been planned by the Junoesque young lady who was breathing down my neck. It was a nice breath and it tickled, but I wasn't so dumb that I didn't think it was meant to.

I told myself sternly that an hour of night-club notoriety had gone to my head. "Be yourself, Brother Douglas," I thought. "You're just a poor, lonely mug that she's sorry for."

Cold logic told me I was wrong. It occurred to me that very recently Miss Livingston had been thrown back into the Cafe Society jungles after paying a half million dollars' ransom money. I was thinking that someone had deposited one hundred thousand dollars to my credit without so much as a by-your-leave. I was thinking that this was the only person I'd ever met who had a hundred thousand in spare cash kicking around.

The thought was fantastic. I tried shoving it out of my mind, but it wouldn't shove. It looked like a third•link in the chain of things that had started happening to me after twenty-eight uneventful years.

Why, for instance, should Candy Livingston present me with one hundred thousand dollars? But then why should she make so obvious a play for me? Why had she asked me to dance instead of grabbing the prize package, which was

53

Ricardo. Why . . . well, why anything? Why, for instance, should a strange young lady named Ethel Brower have strolled into my apartment and got strangled?

Candy said, "Why did you shake your head just then?"

I said, "Did I?"

"Yes. You were thinking of something else. What was it?"

"What do men usually think when you dance with them?"

"You weren't thinking *that*."

"I don't know what I was thinking really. So it couldn't have been important."

"Maybe," she suggested, "you were wondering why I've been working on you."

"Maybe."

"Try the simple answer. Perhaps I think you're cute."

"More likely," I said, "you enjoy proving that you're irresistible."

I stopped dancing, wrapped my fingers around her arm and guided her toward our table. She said, "Hard to get, eh? We'll see." She smiled when she said it, but I knew she wasn't kidding.

Before she could sit down, Ricardo swung into action. Would Miss Livingston honor him? Miss Livingston would. I held out my hand to Dana, who had completed her chore with the nice young man at her left. "It's got to happen one time," I said. "This may as well be it."

We shoved into the crowd. And this time we shoved. People weren't standing back any more to look at me. They were staring at Candy and Ricardo. Dana and I had to fight for every inch. She said, "What goes on here?"

"Meaning . . . ?"

"You and Candy."

"Oh, *that!* You should understand. I'm a big ol' he-man. Take one look at me and get ants in your dance."

"I don't," stated Dana flatly, "but Miss Livingston does."

"And did I eat it up! You have no idea how important I felt."

Dana said thoughtfully, "Let's be serious. I got the idea that it was you she wanted all the time. She saw you with Ricardo and me, and that made the approach simple. We're always being invited to join people. That's why I so often use

54

the exit through the other building. Anyway, she's been concentrating on you ever since we joined her. Or am I wrong?"

"Shall I be modest or honest?"

"Try honesty. It won't hurt much."

"Okay. Admitting that I'm a combination of Adonis, Hercules, and Frank Sinatra, it still came too fast. And she gave me a definite idea that she intended to see me again."

A troubled frown appeared on Dana's forehead. "I was thinking it might be that way. The play tonight has been too obvious. It looked planned. At first I thought I was letting jealousy work on me, but then I knew that wasn't it. I thought of the bank deposit . . . then I realized that was absurd. She didn't know you then."

"And I don't know Ethel Brower even yet."

Dana said, "There's something going on I neither understand nor like."

"Maybe. Maybe not. We're both letting hunches push us around. Just because two inexplicable things have happened to me, we've got no right to tie other things in with them."

"But you still feel it, don't you?"

I said, "Look, sweetheart—of course I do. But common sense tells me I'm wrong."

"I don't believe you are. I have a feeling that these things are all wrapped up in the same package."

I saw she was worried and tried to rally her. She said, "I can't laugh about it, Kirk. And believe me, it isn't jealousy. Not that I couldn't be jealous of someone who can offer what she can. But this is a different feeling. I'm afraid."

"Of what?"

"I don't know."

I said, "What should I do . . . presuming Candy continues to play interested?"

"What could you do?"

"I could tell her—in a nice, polite way, of course—to go peddle her apples somewhere else. Or I could string along and try to find out what's behind it. You tell me."

The orchestra finished the set, and started to make way for the rhumba band. Dana and I went back to the table. Miss Livingston said things to the head waiter and a few minutes later two bottles of champagne appeared along with seven hollow-stemmed glasses. I'd have preferred a slice of rare roast beef and a baked potato, but if they forced champagne on me I figured I'd better grin and bear it.

The evening moved along. Candy brushed off Ricardo's overtures and ignored her trio of escorts. That left Dana with her hands full, and Ricardo more than a trifle bewildered.

Candy concentrated on me. She asked a million questions. She found out everything about me except that I was in love with Dana. That was something I couldn't very well volunteer, seeing that Dana's husband was sitting right there at the table. Candy undoubtedly thought that I was in the public domain. She didn't seem to care who knew that she had found herself a new playtoy.

I tried to live up to her. I didn't cover myself with glory. My conversation was as bright and gay as the tread of an elephant. I can play cute for just so long, then my line runs out.

At midnight Ricardo and Dana excused themselves and went to dress for the supper show. After-theater guests were commencing to pour in. The head waiters assumed new dignity. Candy got me out on the floor again and put a Q.E.D. on the theorem that two can dance closer than one.

She kept up a continuous chatter during the time the show was on, except when Ricardo & Dana were performing. By the time they rejoined us, I knew several things.

I knew that Candy Livingston wanted me to believe that I was the really big moment in her life.

I knew that she intended to see me again—soon and alone.

I was convinced that there was method to her madness, and that it was up to me to find out what it was.

IX

THE NEXT day—Wednesday—started like any other day. There was nothing in the chilly air of a gloomy morning to tell me that something unusual was about to happen. Something unusual and very, very nice.

I entered the office building and rode up to the eighteenth

floor in a big elevator which was all gray and chromium. I always felt important riding in one of those cages. I felt even more important when I entered the reception room of Yarborough & Jensen—Architects. That was where I worked. I was worth one hundred dollars a week to them.

You've got to have something on the ball to maintain a suite like the Yarborough & Jensen layout. It occupied about one-third of the entire floor. There was this reception room, approximately half as large as the Grand Canyon. There was a cool, confident, not unattractive receptionist sitting at a little desk on which was a PBX and an office intercom. There was a very young office boy who was astonishingly polite. Both said good morning and both stàred at me. I wondered whether they knew I'd been dancing with Candy Livingston the night before or whether their interest still sprang from the fact that a young lady had been murdered in my apartment. I bet myself a new hat that they'd gasp if they knew I had one hundred thousand dollars in the bank, not counting the seven hundred that really belonged to me.

Off the reception room were the private offices of the two bosses; a luxurious conference room which reeked of affluence. There was another room which was stocked with sketches, blueprints, plans and specifications. There was a small storeroom full of the things that journeymen architects require. Finally there was a huge, brilliantly lighted room, studded with high tables on which were drawing boards and drafting instruments. That was where I worked. That was also where eleven other young architects struggled to earn their weekly stipends.

The firm was dazzlingly successful. What's more, it was good. Some day, perhaps, I'd want to work somewhere else, at better pay. It would do me good in the profession to be able to refer my prospective employer to Yarborough & Jensen.

I pulled up a high stool, and started in where I'd left off the previous day. A couple of the other boys were already at work. Others were drifting in. A nice, intelligent, competent crowd. We said good morning all around. There wasn't any supervision. We had our jobs to do, and the chiefs were pretty sure that we'd do them the best we knew how.

At a few minutes after eleven the telephone rang. One of the boys answered and called across to me, "For you, Douglas. A Dr. Arthur Maybank."

I wiped my ruling pen on a piece of chamois, clambered down from my stool, said thank you, and picked up the phone. Arthur's mild, meek voice came to me over the wire.

"Kirk?"

"Yes."

"Listen, this is important. I want you to have lunch with me today."

He seemed excited. I said, "Sure. Something special?"

"Nothing you're thinking about. Can you stay away from the office for a long time? Two or three hours maybe?"

I hesitated. He went on eagerly. "It's in line with your work," he said. "I'd rather not explain over the phone. I want to surprise you."

"Okay," I told him. "When and where?"

He said 12:30 would be about right. He named the men's grill of a swank Park Avenue hotel. He said, "Pretty yourself up, Kirk. There's somebody you've got to impress."

"Not a woman."

"Good Lord! No."

I told Oliver Jensen about the call. He told me to stay as long as I wanted. There was a twinkle in his eyes when he advised me to fancy myself up. I wondered whether he had heard about last night at the Club Caliente. He seemed to be kidding me without saying a word.

At 12:30 on the dot I shoved through a revolving door and entered the grill. I loaned my coat and hat to the checkroom girl. I looked across the room and spotted Arthur. He was sitting in a very choice alcove, at a table which had set-ups for three, and he wasn't alone. He was with a man.

They didn't see me, and so I had plenty of time to size up Arthur's friend as I crossed toward them. One thing I knew for sure: this was one of the handsomest men I had ever seen.

I guessed him to be about forty-two years old, six feet tall and weighing perhaps 175. He had a fine face, strong features, and a head of iron-gray hair which gave him a distinguished appearance. He was wearing a quiet salt-and-pepper tweed. He had on a gray shirt and a plain blue necktie. He was

58

listening to something Arthur was saying, his quiet gray eyes intent on the face of the young interne.

I stopped at the table and Arthur leaped to his feet. The stranger rose, too. Arthur said, "Mr. Ferguson—may I present my friend, Kirk Douglas? Kirk—Mr. John Ferguson."

We shook hands. Ferguson had a strong grip and level eyes. We stated that we were pleased to meet one another, he nodded at a chair and we all sat down.

While waiting to be served, John Ferguson broke the conversational ice. He said, "The doctor, here, seems rather fond of you, Mr. Douglas."

I grinned at Arthur and he beamed. He said, "I met Mr. Ferguson at the hospital. He was getting rid of an appendix and I used to help the nurse take his temperature."

"You also," reminded Ferguson with a smile, "used to slip into my room and play chess when you weren't too busy."

"And," confessed Arthur, "sometimes when I was."

The waiter came with our lunches. I knew that Ferguson was estimating me, though why, I hadn't the slightest idea. Finally he said, "You're an architect, aren't you, Mr. Douglas?"

"Yes. I work for Yarborough & Jensen."

"Excellent firm." He ate silently for a moment, then flashed me a charming smile. "This will probably strike you as unusual, but Maybank's enthusiasm is responsible."

I waited. He went on: "I am planning the construction of an important office building. Not myself alone: a group of us. The building will not be in New York. We own a choice corner in a large city: 100 by 120. We want the most beautiful 25-story building in America to be constructed on that site. We can get high rentals. Maybank tells me that you've made a special study of that sort of design, and that you have some interesting ideas."

I said, "That's right, Mr. Ferguson. But Arthur isn't qualified to state whether my ideas are any good."

"True. I'd like to find out for myself. Meanwhile, I wondered whether it would be incorrect procedure for me to talk to one of the firm members, and to request that you be assigned to the job? Naturally, your ideas might not check with

59

mine. If I thought you couldn't offer what I want, I'd be frank with you."

My heart did a double somersault. This was the sort of break every young employee of a big firm prays for. Of course, if I tackled the assignment and flopped on it, I'd be in the doghouse. But if I could give this man what he wanted . . . That was an important job, even for a firm like mine.

I didn't attempt to take it in stride. I explained quite honestly—and enthusiastically—what it would mean to me. I was as excited as a kid. I thanked Arthur for what he had done. I was thinking about how sometimes bread cast on the waters returned in the form of angel cake. If a job like this had been laid in my lap years from then, I'd have been thrilled. Coming this way . . . the office getting it through me and with a request of the client that I be assigned . . . that meant plenty.

Mr. Ferguson and I started talking. He knew what he wanted. Most of his ideas were sound. He asked me questions and listened patiently while I talked. Every once in a while he'd nod. Occasionally he'd object. But on the basic essentials we saw eye to eye.

I forgot Arthur Maybank. I forgot him until I saw him standing up and heard him saying he had to get back to the McKinley. He seemed delighted at having been able to do me this favor, but I was sure he didn't understand what a tremendous favor it was. I felt badly for having ignored him, after all, I owed this break to him.

He stood at the table, saying good bye to Ferguson. He looked seedy and shy. I said, "Working tonight, Arthur?"

"I'm off at seven."

"I'll pick you up at the hospital. We'll have a celebration dinner together.

Arthur Maybank vanished. Ferguson and I started talking again. After a while, he paid the check and we walked back to my office. I introduced him to Jensen. I said I'd prefer to have them talk privately. I went into the drafting room and perched on my high stool and stared at the New York skyline and let myself float. An opportunity like this! A chance to go far places fast! I put my elbows on the drawing board and crossed two fingers on each hand.

It was three o'clock before Jensen and Ferguson reappeared. Jensen looked as though he had swallowed the canary. They walked over to where I was sitting and the boss said he was handing it to me. He said, "But you'd better not give this firm a black eye, Douglas," and I said I'd try not to.

Ferguson left. I attempted to work, but didn't make any progress. I saw Yarborough go into his partner's office, and later he came out and walked over to my desk. He congratulated me. He got a report on the work I was doing and told me he was taking it off my hands. I was to confine myself to this one job. He suggested that I talk things over with him or Mr. Jensen. He cautioned against too great haste, reminding me that major construction couldn't be started for a long time to come. He was quite cordial. I was, too, but I was in a fog.

I telephoned Dana. The cleaning maid answered and told me she was out: rehearsing. I wanted to tell her all about it. I wanted to strut. I was scared and confident all at the same time.

I scrubbed myself at the office. I went straight from there to the McKinley Hospital. I walked through the same dingy entrance into the same dingy accident room Dana and I had visited not so long ago. The girls on duty were different girls, but just as disinterested. I circled the glass cage and went into the white-tiled room with the half dozen surgical wagons in it, and the row of steel lockers showing through the doorway. I saw Arthur Maybank talking to a cop. The policeman had a notebook and pencil and he was jotting things down. Arthur saw me and waved. He called brightly, "Be with you in a minute. Make yourself uncomfortable."

I amused myself by watching them bring an accident case in. A tall, thin, boyish-looking interne took charge. I took a look at the patient and promptly wished I hadn't. By that time the cop and Arthur had finished. The cop walked out, and Arthur joined me. He was dressed for the street.

I hailed a taxi and we jumped in. I gave the address of the Club Caliente. It wasn't new to Arthur—he'd been there with me a dozen times—but I knew it was always a thrill.

61

We started across town and he said, "I hated to keep you waiting, Kirk . . . but it was one of those things."

"What sort of things?"

"Accident stuff. We get policemen in our hair all the time. This man was investigating a hit-and-run case. Guy got hit in Central Park the night of the blizzard. Nobody saw it happen. Nobody saw the car that did it. I was on ambulance duty and made the run. The call had come in from a passing motorist who saw the man lying in the snow. I brought him in—he was somebody named Norton—and gave him a saline infusion in the accident room, and some plasma. A few minutes after we got him into the operating room he died."

I said, "What did the policeman want?"

"More information. He's from the motor homicide squad, and those babies are hell on hit-and-run stuff. They hate it worse than poison, and hang on like bulldogs. The patient was conscious in the ambulance, and talked to me some. The cop wanted to know what he said. They've never found the car that did it, and they won't rest until they do. If they find him . . ." Arthur made an expressive gesture. "I'd hate to be the driver, that's all."

"You get much of that?"

"All the time. It's part of the job. Let's forget it."

I was willing enough. I started telling Arthur how grateful I was for introducing me to John Ferguson. He bloomed under my thanks. "We talked a lot when he was a patient," Arthur explained. "He told me about this idea of his, and I started popping off about you. All I did was bring you together."

I piled it on as thick as I could. I said, "Maybe some day when I'm rich and famous I'll meet an important man who wants an especially large operation, Arthur, and I'll steer him up against you. And when it's over, I'll still owe you a million thanks."

We ran into Dana and Ricardo in the lobby of the club. They both looked like thunderclouds. Dance teams rehearse all the time, and they quarrel while they're doing it. It's agony to them. Dana & Ricardo were not different from any of the other topflight dance teams in that way.

I bought a glass of sherry for Dana. I dragged her back to

my special table. I told her about the break I'd got, and I put the credit where it was due. Arthur was happy. Dana snapped out of her black mood. She wanted to know all about it. She made me believe that she was more interested in office buildings than anything else in the world. She told Arthur he was wonderful. She had him glowing like a firefly by the time she rushed to her dressing room to fix up for the dinner show.

Arthur looked at me and said, "For God's sake, Kirk—why don't you marry her?"

"No can do," I answered. "Bigamy isn't one of my vices."

"But look—it doesn't make sense. You're crazy about each other. She isn't really Ricardo's wife. There must be some way."

Arthur was plunging into a subject I didn't often discuss—perhaps because I had thought about it so much. The fact that I talked lightly didn't mean that I hadn't spent lots of sleepless nights worrying.

All my thinking hadn't ever got me anywhere. There had been times when I'd been so depressed by the hopelessness of the situation that I'd blame Dana. Then I'd come to my senses and start blaming myself. And that wasn't good, either.

I said, "I wish I could find the answer. It isn't as simple as it looks. You've been around here enough to know that Dana is two people: she's Dana, the nice kid: and Dana, the dancer. She's half of Ricardo & Dana, and that means plenty."

"Marrying you," he insisted stubbornly, "wouldn't break up the act. She could go on dancing with him—or would you object?"

"Don't be silly. Of course I wouldn't. It's a big part of her life. The point is that Ricardo doesn't see it that way. He promises that he'll get her a divorce when and if he finds a new partner. Or, in answer to the statement that he isn't trying to find one, he says he'll turn her loose at some indefinite future date. And he swears he'll fight any divorce action she might bring."

Arthur said, "In this State there's only one legal cause. Infidelity. Do you mean to tell me that Ricardo doesn't play around?"

63

"He may. But if he does, he's discreet. We've never caught him at it."

Arthur said, with a violence surprising for so diffident a person, "I don't like him. His slant isn't normal. It's sadistic."

"The result is the same."

"But your attitude ought to be different. I think the man gets a kick out of keeping you two apart."

"You may be right. But suppose it were possible to push over the applecart: that wouldn't be much of a way to start a successful marriage, would it?"

"You're too damned high-minded, that's what's the matter with you, Kirk. If I were in love with a girl like that, and she was in love with me, I'd do whatever I had to do to get her."

"Suppose there's nothing you could do?"

He made an impatient gesture. "Are you proposing to take it on the chin indefinitely?"

"I don't know. That sounds spineless, but it happens to be true. Ricardo would fight any divorce action she might bring. He'd block her. Then we'd be worse off than we are now."

"Why?"

I said slowly, "If necessary, he'd file a countersuit. He'd defend by charging her with infidelity. Neither Dana nor I would like that."

"I get it . . ." Arthur gripped the edge of the table. "But it's rotten. And since I'm shooting off my mouth, I'll tell you something else. I do more than dislike Ricardo. I'm afraid of him."

"Afraid?"

"Not for me. For you. The man hates your guts. He's suave on the surface, but he wouldn't stop at anything. You take my advice, Kirk—and keep your guard up."

I said, "You're driving at something. What is it?"

Arthur leaned across the table. His pale, weak eyes bored into mine. "Think this over," he said. "Try to figure what it might add up to if Ricardo was still in love with Dana."

I said, "I don't quite follow."

"All right, I'll draw a picture for you. Suppose he's still in love with her. It's not impossible, you know. And if that's how it is, try to figure how he feels when he sees her with

64

you, when he is reminded day after day and night after night that she is in love with you. Suppose . . . ah! forget it."

"Go ahead, Arthur. Please."

"All right, I will. Suppose he were brooding over it. Suppose he went to your apartment and found a woman there. Suppose he thought it was Dana. Suppose he killed her."

I said, "It couldn't have happened that way."

"The apartment was dark when they got there, wasn't it?"

"Yes . . ."

"Then it could have happened like that."

I was silent for perhaps a minute. Then I said, "You're crazy."

He looked at me and shook his head. He didn't say anything.

I thought, "Sure, he's crazy."

And then I thought, "But suppose he's not . . ."

X

WE'D PROBABLY have continued the conversation indefinitely, except that somebody came in. It was John Ferguson. He was wearing a business suit of midnight blue which looked black. He looked very handsome, and he was alone.

The head waiter started to put him at a corner table, gave him a second look, and seated him instead at a choice table. Ferguson said something—probably he ordered a cocktail— and the head waiter walked off importantly.

The orchestras were changing. Almost time for the dinner show. Ferguson glanced around the half-empty room. Obviously, he knew the place. He spotted us, and didn't hesitate. He came over, and asked whether we wouldn't join him for dinner. He had a nice manner, but it was a manner that wasn't accustomed to having No said to it. So we said Yes. I was tickled, because it was Ferguson, but at the same time I wondered what Dana would think. We weren't having much luck being alone these days.

The head waiter appeared again as we approached the little wall table. John Ferguson said he wanted a larger one, at the ringside. We got a table right smack on the floor. Arthur and I ordered dry Martinis and inspected the menu. Arthur reacted as he always did when I brought him to the Caliente. His eyes bugged out at the price list. He ordered the cheapest item among the entrees. It was still expensive from the standpoint of a young M.D. who was interning at nothing a month.

The music blared, and the scantily-clad chorus girls cavorted onto the small, polished floor. Arthur didn't miss a trick. His capacity for enjoying things that other men took for granted was enormous. Ferguson regarded him gravely for a moment, then looked at me and smiled. I smiled, too. We were sharing Arthur's fun. It made me like Ferguson even better than I had before.

The girls trotted off and the emcee announced the singer. He placed the microphone for her. And just as she started, there came from the door the identifiable sound of scurrying that meant a celebrity was entering. The celebrity was Candy Livingston. Again she was accompanied by three people, but this time only two of them were men. One of the men was obviously attached to the coldly attractive girl whose arm he held.

They conducted Miss Livingston to the table next to ours. They pushed things around and made a lot of noise. The singer kept on singing, but she wasn't having much fun. She wasn't getting much attention, either. She glared at Candy. Miss Livingston didn't seem to mind.

She sat down facing us. Then she got up immediately. She came over and held out her hand. She looked at my companions and I did the honors: "Miss Livingston, may I present Mr. Ferguson and Dr. Maybank?" She smiled at both and said, "This is ridiculous. We'll make it one big happy family."

The singer continued to suffer while the waiters made a lot more noise shoving two tables together. Candy said something to the head man, and I guessed she was telling him that she wished to pay the freight. I wondered how Ferguson was taking it. He looked amused—nothing more. But Arthur Maybank was way up yonder where the air is thin. Sitting

66

at the table with Candy Livingston! I could almost hear him thinking, "Oh, boy! It this something!"

Candy seemed somewhat less than fascinated by the show. She introduced her friends. Their party of four was now a party of seven, but they didn't appear to be surprised. I had an idea that if you played around with Candy Livingston long enough you'd become accustomed to anything.

Ricardo & Dana came on. Candy was saying something to me when the act commenced, but I pointedly didn't answer. She gave me a quick look, but she took the hint and put the brakes on her conversation while the act was on. After the customary three numbers there was a lot of applause. Poised by the bandstand, I fancied that Dana caught a glimpse of me—and of Candy Livingston. I thought I saw a little frown on her forehead, but before I could be sure they were dancing again.

As soon as they took their bows, Candy called the captain and ordered two more places set. She got up and said she'd be back in a minute. She disappeared through the door back of the bandstand. She returned in fifteen minutes with Ricardo and Dana in tow. It was my idea that Dana looked somewhat less than happy, but she brightened up when I introduced her to John Ferguson. She caught the name and the implication instantly, and started devoting herself to him. I gazed at her with admiration, thinking what a perfect wife she'd make for a rising young architect. When better office buildings were built, she'd help him build 'em.

We ordered dinner and started to eat it. The table was pretty crowded, but nobody seemed to mind. I was having a good time, and Arthur Maybank was purring. He wasn't case-hardened. Celebrities were a novelty to him. And here he was at the table with Dana Warren, Ricardo Sanchez and Candy Livingston. What more could a man ask for his memory book?

I got most of my fun by watching him. I saw a girl staring at him from one of the wall tables. She caught his eye and smiled and nodded. Arthur nodded right back, but he looked rather vague. A few minutes later the performance was repeated.

I took a second look. The girl was a good deal older than

67

Arthur—my guess was about thirty-three—but she could have been any age. She had a nice, olive skin and deep black eyes. Black hair was smartly done over a well-shaped head. She was as sleek and correct as something out of a fashion magazine. I said to Arthur, "Hi, Lothario—who's the girl?"

He flushed with embarrassment and pride. "I couldn't spot her at first," he said, "but I think I do—now."

"She seems to like you."

He shook his head shyly. "Maybe she's impressed by the people I'm with." He nodded as though to confirm his own beliefs. "That's who she is. I got it now."

"Is it a secret?"

"She's a nurse's aide at the McKinley. I'm sure of it."

"But not positive?"

"We-e-ell, yes, I am. Sort of."

Ten minutes later I said, "She's still giving you the eye, Arthur. Why not grab a dance for yourself?"

"Oh, no! I don't even know her name. And she isn't alone."

"At least," I said, "I'd go speak to her if I were you. Maybe she'd like her gentleman friend to be impressed."

It took a bit of arguing, but he went over while they were taking off the dinner plates and inquiring what we'd like for dessert.

I saw him go to the wall table and speak to the girl. She put everything she had into the smile she gave him. He seated himself gingerly on a chair he captured from an adjoining table. I liked what was happening. For my money, this was Arthur Maybank's night, and if he was having fun, so was I.

A little while later he and the girl got up and started for the dance floor. He looked appalled by what was happening. I winked at him and that seemed to boost his morale.

He didn't dance badly. The vivid young lady with him sparkled at him all through the dance. Arthur looked beatific. Something new had been added—and he liked it.

After a long while, they quit. He brought her to our table. He introduced her all around. She was Miss Agnes Sheridan. She seemed particularly delighted to meet Candy Livingston.

We men were all standing up. We shook hands with her in turn. Ricardo, and then Candy's young men, then me, and finally John Ferguson. We said the usual things in the usual

68

way. John Ferguson smiled at Arthur. He said, "You get around, don't you, Maybank?" It was a nice touch.

Arthur took her back to her table, chatted a few moments and then left her. I started kidding him about his conquest, and he blushed. He said, "Aw, lay off, Kirk. She's been a nurse's aide at the McKinley for months and she never noticed me until she saw me with Miss Livingston."

"You're too modest, Arthur. She might have been interested in Miss Livingston, but she likes you."

We had a lot of fun. We sat around and talked and danced occasionally, and drank wine. Arthur tried another session on the floor with Miss Sheridan. Whatever it was that was brewing there, seemed to be brewing fast.

I dragged Arthur away before the supper show. He wanted to stay but I reminded him that he'd be on duty at seven the next morning. I also reminded myself that I was now an important architect and needed a clear head for heavy thinking. Candy wanted to know whether I'd give her a call, or whether she'd have to start acting like a hussy. As we shouldered our way out, Miss Agnes Sheridan smiled and waved at Arthur, and he waved back. I took him to the McKinley in a taxi. He said, "Kirk, I never had so much fun in my life. Never."

Thursday I worked. I got hold of a lot of books and started reading. I absorbed a lot of dope about office buildings. A glittering opportunity had been laid in my lap and I didn't propose to muff it.

Friday was a busy day, too. I had a couple of conferences with a contractor who was doing an alteration job on a big apartment house. It was something I'd been handling before the Ferguson job turned up. When I finished with him, I telephoned Dana's apartment. She was rehearsing again. She was always rehearsing. Dance teams work so smoothly on the floor. Since I'd met Dana, I'd found out why. They kill themselves acquiring that perfection.

I went home and settled myself for another evening of research. I poured myself a drink and sat down with the evening paper. The bell rang and I let Arthur Maybank in. He started talking about inconsequential things, but I knew he had something on his mind.

Finally I got it. He had a date with Agnes Sheridan for

that night. He was broke and wanted to borrow twenty dollars. You'd have thought he was asking me for the United States mint.

I tried to make it more than that, but he insisted that twenty was enough. He said he wouldn't be embarrassed with Miss Sheridan because she knew what his job was. He was asking for twenty, he said, because he thought it would be fun to take her back to the Club Caliente. I caught it, all right. In the Caliente, Arthur knew people. He was a big shot.

I said, "You're sure making time, son."

"She's awfully nice."

"Did you see her yesterday?"

"Well, yes . . . I managed to. In fact, we had lunch together."

I grinned. "Better watch your step. You're slipping."

He answered shyly, "I guess every man's entitled to be a damn fool one time, isn't he?"

He went away. He had my twenty dollars and he was walking on air.

Saturday night I got to the club early. I felt as though I hadn't seen Dana since forever. I said, "This is a hell of a note: Just because I'm on the way to become a successful architect, I don't see you any more." I held her at arm's length. "You've become infinitely more beautiful in the past three days, darling."

She said, "How's the work going?"

"Not too fast. But tonight I'm forgetting it. Let's find a quiet place for dinner between shows and talk about us."

She thought that was a good idea. And then she said, "But I do wish you'd been in last night. Arthur was here with that Miss Sheridan, and she was cute."

"In what way?"

"In every way. She either likes him or she's giving a reasonable facsimile thereof. And he shows all the symptoms of a gent who has fallen hard."

"I'm not questioning his side of it," I said. "But how about Miss Sheridan's? Is she impressed by Arthur or by his friends?"

"Both, I think. Maybe it was just the friends at first, but now he seems to have emerged as a personality."

70

"That's not easy to imagine. He isn't what you'd call color-ful."

"That's the nicest thing about him."

I said, "Did you speak to them?"

"Of course. I sat at their table. So did Candy Livingston."

"So she was in again, eh?"

"Yes, indeed. She seemed slightly heartbroken at not find-ing you here. How's it getting along, by the way?"

I said, "Be yourself, Beautiful. My relationship with Miss Livingston is strictly a night-club affair."

Dana looked at me oddly. She said, "Maybe." Then she vanished into the corridor which led to her dressing room. I sat by myself, watched her act with the usual detached feeling that annoyed me, and waited while she changed into street clothes. When she joined me again, she was ready to go. Just as we started out, a page boy came up and wanted to know whether I was Mr. Douglas. I said I was, and he said, "Somebody wants you on the phone."

Dana and I followed the kid to the lobby, so that when I'd finished talking, we could escape quickly. It was already half past ten. I picked up the phone and Dana and I looked at each other. We hadn't said a word, but each knew what the other was thinking. Fifty to one, it was Candy Livingston. But it wasn't. It was a voice I'd never heard before: a woman's voice. It was harsh, penetrating. It said, "Mr. Douglas?"

"Yes."

"McKinley Hospital speaking. You're a friend of Dr. Arthur Maybank, ain't you?"

"Yes."

"Well, maybe you better come over here."

I didn't like the way she said it. I put my lips close against the mouthpiece and asked, "Is it important, Miss?"

"I'll say it is." The voice held more than a trace of excite-ment. "Dr. Maybank has just been shot."

XI

I WAS THINKING fast when I came out of the phone booth.
To tell Dana or not to tell her, that was the question. I decided I'd better. She'd find out soon enough, anyway.

She took it standing up. She drew in her breath sharply
and her eyes got wide. She said, "Something else?" and I
knew what she meant. I was thinking the same thing.

We walked out of the club and stood on the curb while the
doorman tried to flag a taxi. It was a tough job because the
night was bad. What had been snow had turned to slush;
what had been rain had become sleet. A freezing wind swept
up from the river and chilled me all the way through.

A taxi swung into the curb and disgorged two men and a
woman. I grabbed the taxi and said, "McKinley Hospital,
and step on it, Bud." We slid and lurched westward. I took
Dana's hand. It was almost as cold as mine.

She asked, "Is he dead?"

"I don't know. That's all the girl said: that he'd been shot."

She didn't ask any more questions. We skidded on dirty
snow through dirty streets. My mind flashed back to Wednesday night: Arthur Maybank having the time of his life, being
somebody in a place where there were a lot of somebodies.
Letting himself go over a woman. Taking her out last night
with my twenty dollars. Stretched out now in his own hospital, victim of a shooting. That's all I knew, but it was
enough to make me feel ill.

We stopped at the curb in front of the main entrance. I
gave the driver a dollar bill and told him to keep the change.
We went into the dingy lobby and spoke to the dingy girl at
the receptionist's desk. We told her we were friends of Dr.
Arthur Maybank and wanted to see him. She jerked her head
toward the old-fashioned iron grillwork of the elevator and
forgot all about us. We went up to the fourth floor.

It was better up there, but still not good. People walked
around, some dressed as we were and some in white. This

72

was a private room floor. So they were treating Arthur all right. I was glad.

A girl approached us. She was slim and dark and had a clear olive complexion. Her black eyes looked frightened. She had on a little hat and a brown dress. The sheared beaver coat she wore was open. That's how I could see the brown dress.

Agnes Sheridan said, "I'm glad you're here. I thought you might be at the club, Mr. Douglas. I suggested they phone you."

I said, "How bad is it?"

"Not bad. But that isn't the point. Somebody shot at him."

"When?"

"Less than an hour ago. I had a date with him. I was in the little restaurant near the corner, and he was supposed to join me there for a cup of coffee and some doughnuts. When he didn't show up, I came over to see what was detaining him. They told me what had happened."

"What did they tell you?"

"That he had slipped his overcoat on over his whites and told the other interne he'd be back in a few minutes. He went across the parking space, and somebody fired at him from among the parked cars."

"Did they catch him?"

"No."

"Has Arthur any idea . . ."

"No. It just happened. He was unconscious, but only for a little while. He was hit in the arm. The resident surgeon says he'll be up and around by tomorrow. But if somebody shot at him deliberately, they might try it again."

I said, "You're really fond of him, aren't you?"

"I like him. He's different from anybody I've ever met."

That made sense. There was a lot of emotion bottled up in this Sheridan woman. She was shaking now, and Dana put a hand on her arm to steady her. Agnes went right on talking, as though it made her feel better to get things off her chest.

"They called the police. The cops talked to him as soon as he came down from the operating room. They left just a few minutes ago."

"Can we see him?"

73

"I think so. I'll ask the hall nurse."

She knew just where she was going. She'd been working at the McKinley quite a while as a nurse's aide. She returned in a few seconds and led us into a room which was clean enough, provided you were too sick to care about details.

Arthur smiled when we came in. It was a brave effort, but not too successful. This wasn't the Arthur of Wednesday night. He looked sick and frightened. There was something behind his eyes that disturbed me, as though he knew that the end was not yet.

Dana went over to the bed and said something nice. He took her hand and said, "Thanks." There was real warmth in the smile he gave Agnes Sheridan.

I asked him how he was feeling and he said, "Fine." He told me it was nothing at all, just a flesh wound in the arm. He said he'd be on the job next day, as usual—or, at the latest, the day after that. He was trying to be the big brave boy, and he wasn't getting away with it.

I pulled up a chair. I asked him to tell me about it. He said, "There isn't much to tell. I was walking across the parking lot. Something hit me. I couldn't even swear I heard the shot. Next thing I knew they were rolling me into the operating room."

I smiled brightly. "Probably an accident."

"I'd like to think so. But I don't."

Dana said, "Why would anybody want to shoot you?"

"I can't figure that one, either. It may have been some screwball who used to be a patient. Maybe someone who took a dislike to me."

"But that isn't what you think, is it?"

"I don't know what to think."

He told me about the cops being there. From his description, they were a couple of detectives from the same division the hospital is in. According to him, they asked all sorts of questions, and promised to stick with it. He said, "But there's nothing to stick with. I couldn't think of anybody who would want to shoot me, so what chance have they got?"

He wasn't badly hurt. But he'd been shaken up plenty. He was jittery. We sat around and talked. We talked mostly about how lucky he was; what an escape he'd had. He agreed

74

with us, but he wasn't happy. He was thinking that there'd likely be a next time, and he might not be so lucky then.

Time passed faster than we knew. Dana looked at her watch and seemed troubled. I said I'd run her back to the club for the supper show. She wouldn't hear of it. Arthur begged Agnes to go home. He was pitifully grateful to her.

She said she intended to stay, but Arthur argued her down. She finally agreed to go with Dana. She'd drop Dana at the club and keep the same taxi. We said good night. Agnes leaned over the bed and brushed her lips over Arthur's. He seemed to like it.

It was almost midnight. Arthur and I were alone. From the corridor came the usual hushed sounds of a hospital. The elevator made the only real noise. Its door banged every time it opened, every time it closed. Arthur didn't seem to notice.

I was feeling lousy. I fumbled for a cigarette, then stowed it away again. Arthur said, "Go ahead. Give me one, too." We lighted up. It seemed to help both of us.

I said, "Is it all right to talk?"

"Sure. I'm okay. Scared—that's all."

I said, "You told the police you didn't have any idea who might have done it. Is that true?"

"Yes. I wish it weren't."

"I don't get it. An attempted murder almost out in the open . . ."

"It was a good safe place." He smiled wanly. "And it's a pretty bad night."

"You didn't see the person who shot at you?"

"No." He hesitated. "That is . . . well, I don't think so."

"What does that mean?"

"Something like that happens, Kirk—and you're liable to remember things that never occurred. While they had me in the operating room I had a hazy remembrance of seeing a man running out from among the parked cars. I'd say a tall man, wearing a felt hat and an overcoat. But I couldn't swear to it. It may have been imagination entirely."

I kept on probing. Maybe there was something important that he wouldn't recognize as important. I asked the questions, but he didn't seem to have the answers. The resident physician came in and chatted with us. He gave Arthur a colorless liquid in a little glass. He said, "That'll give you a good night's rest." Then he suggested that I probably needed some sleep, it being already two o'clock.

I told Arthur I'd see him the first thing the next morning. He said there wasn't anything he wanted. I hoped the medicine was going to knock him cold. I didn't want him to lie awake all night with nothing but his thoughts for company.

I walked to my apartment. I undressed and slipped under the covers. I kept the light on and lay there for a while, staring at the ceiling.

At three o'clock I telephoned Dana's apartment. She answered so quickly that I knew she must have been waiting for the call. Her voice was far from steady. I told her Arthur was right as rain. I said that it might have been an accident. I didn't press that point too far, because then she wouldn't have believed me. I just planted the idea.

She asked me things which I couldn't answer. I told her if she weren't able to sleep she must call me. She promised. We said good night and hung up. I felt more lonely, more worried, than ever.

Facts were marching around in my brain like little wooden soldiers. They added up to one unpleasant conclusion.

Several inexplicable things had happened recently.

Some unknown person had deposited one hundred thousand dollars to my credit at the bank.

A woman named Ethel Brower, whom I had never seen nor heard of, had been murdered in my apartment.

A very spectacular young lady named Candy Livingston had returned from being kidnaped and had apparently made a deliberate effort to impress herself on me.

Dr. Arthur Maybank had been shot at—probably, but not certainly—by a man who obviously had intended to kill him.

Four major happenings without rhyme or reason. Four occurrences which had only one thing in common.

That thing was me. My bank account, my apartment, my personality, my friend. I felt certain that Arthur had been shot simply because he was a friend of mine. It made no sense. But there it was. I, Kirk Douglas, was the common denominator.

I turned out the light and knew I wouldn't sleep.

76

I also knew that the answer to the puzzle was a long way off. I remembered a line written by a war correspondent. I felt that it fitted this situation.

The line was:

"Things will get much worse before they get better."

XII

SATURDAY to Monday can be a long time, if you've got things to do.

I spent most of Sunday with Arthur Maybank. He was up and about and all ready to start punching the timeclock again Monday morning. He was still jittery and still didn't have any idea about who fired at him or why. We tossed the ball back and forth until we both got tired. There wasn't a single conclusion in a carload of words.

In my spare time I was with Dana. That meant a lot more conversation about the queer things that had been happening. I tried to work and gave it up as a bad job. I was more on edge than I knew. When I didn't sleep Sunday night, I realized I'd better do something. What I did was to telephone Dana at the lunch hour Monday.

I told her it was time for us to snap back to normal. I suggested a between-shows supper at my apartment that night. A nifty little meal that I could whip up. She seemed to like the idea, and we both promised solemnly that we'd wrap up all the words we knew which were synonymous with murder and shove 'em back in the dictionary. This was to be fun. It sounded swell when I thought it up. It sounded even better as night approached.

She was coming over in a taxi the minute she finished the dinner show. She was going back just in time to put her make-up on and slip into an evening gown. That added up to two hours we'd have together; maybe fifteen minutes more than that.

I shopped on the way home from the office, being careful to buy only things I knew I could cook. That meant lamb chops. I'm a bearcat with those. I bought a few flowers to

77

pretty up the table. I stopped at the liquor store and bought a bottle of a domestic red wine which I knew by experience. It was good wine in anybody's language.

I set up the gateleg table in the middle of the floor and put the flowers on it. I stuck candles in two glass candlesticks. I figured that would be the payoff. House lights out, flickering glow of candles casting shadows on the wall. Maybe the night wasn't made for love, but I intended to help all I could.

I opened a can of asparagus, which is one of the neatest culinary tricks I know. I fished around in the cupboard and retrieved a tiny glass of genuine Russian caviar. I had saved it for a special occasion, and this was going to be extra special. I got out my wooden salad bowl and started tossing up a green salad. I had some chopped hard-boiled eggs to go with the caviar, a stick of butter, some bakery rolls, my imitation silver and my best napery. I laid off cooking the lamb chops until after the cocktails had been served. If they weren't just right, the whole thing fell down.

Housework doesn't come easy to me. I puttered around in shirt sleeves and a cute little apron Dana had given me. It was half past nine before I caught up with myself. I lighted my pipe and relaxed. Nothing to do now but watch the clock crawl toward ten. Then it would be me and Dana. No murders, no hundred thousand dollars. Just a pretty girl and a mug trying to prove they were in love with each other. We hadn't had an evening like that in so long I'd almost forgotten how lovely it could be.

At 9:40 on the dot, the buzzer sounded. Dana was early. Maybe she'd persuaded them to put on the dance act in the middle of the show. She must have worked some sort of miracle or she couldn't be here this early.

She wasn't. I opened the door and let my jaw drop as I looked into Candy's sapphire eyes.

She had on a coat which could have been mink but which I'm willing to bet was sable. She was wearing a big, floppy green hat. She had on alligator shoes and carried an alligator bag. The coat was open, and I saw she was wearing a green woollen dress. It fitted her snugly enough so you didn't have to strain your imagination.

She stood staring at me, and I did the same right back at

her. Then it hit me that I was forgetting all my party manners. I opened the door a little wider, stood back and said, "Miss Livingston, I presume."

She walked in, took off her coat and hat with a single gesture and flung them on a chair. She took a look at the table, at the foolish little apron I was wearing. She said, in her low, husky, exciting voice, "So *that's* how it is."

I said, "Have a seat. I'm doing things with the cocktail shaker which might turn out to be Manhattans. How about one?"

She glanced at the mantel clock. I could see her brain working. Near the witching hour of ten. Dinner in the process of preparation. I knew she knew it couldn't be anybody but Dana Warren.

She said, "I thought I'd come up and see you sometime. But I picked the wrong time."

I said, "Don't be absurd. I'm delighted."

"Not very convincing. But before I go, tell me: Why don't I get a break like this?"

I grabbed onto that "before I go" business. I hoped she was serious. I said, "What would you be wanting with it?"

"I could use it. It appeals to the domestic in me, plus other things. I'm also quite expert in a kitchen, believe it or not."

I said, "We'll get together—soon."

She gave me a slow smile. "Not quite definite enough, Kirk. What are you: A man or a mice?"

"A mice."

"Then I'll diagram it for you. I, Candy Livingston, being of sound mind and body . . . not a bad body either, if I may say so . . . do solemnly state . . . That's all mixed up. The idea is that I've been throwing myself at you. And you haven't given me a tumble."

"I'm shy."

"Sure. This stage-setting proves it." She made a motion toward her coat and hat. "I'm on my way. My telephone number is in the book. Try using it sometime."

The buzzer sounded again. two short rings, a pause, then a short ring. Too late for anything now. That was Dana.

As I went to the door, I heard Candy say, "I'm sorry . . ." I opened the door and Dana came in. She had her coat over

79

her arm. She was wearing a cute little dress; a sort of blue-and-gray plaid effect. Over her formal hair-do she had thrown a kerchief. She swept into the room and got an eyeful of Candy Livingston.

It would have been funny if I hadn't been so miserable. This was the topper. This was all I needed to make me certain that a black cat was living on the path I was walking. The two girls looked at each other, and then Dana moved across the room with her hand out. You'd have thought that this was the most wonderful thing that ever happened to her.

They shook hands, said nice things about each other, and then Candy said, "I crashed a party. I'm checking out."

"You're doing nothing of the sort." Dana smiled at me. It was a lovely smile with icicles on it. "Have you enough for three, Kirk, or will each of us be one-third starved?"

I said miserably that I had plenty for three. I fled into the kitchen. I slammed the cocktail shaker around, took down a third glass, poured the drinks, put them on a tray and brought them in. I was thinking, "Don't be a damned fool, Dana. She wants to go. Let her do it."

But Dana had other ideas. She was putting herself out to be gracious and lovely. The play had been taken away from me. From here out, I was just the cook.

I went into the kitchen, turned up the flame under the coffee percolator and started pitching lamb chops under the broiler. They sizzled and sputtered, and I hoped some of the fat would jump up and bite me. Then Dana would be sorry!

I heard them arguing. The conventional thing. Candy said she wanted to go. Dana said No. She made it convincing. Maybe she wanted to create the impression that three made her happier than two. It made sense but it didn't make me happy.

We nibbled the caviar while the chops were doing their stuff. Dana didn't even give me a look to indicate that this wasn't just what she would have chosen if she'd had the chance. Romance for two had become boredom for three.

The chops made a lot of smoke. I cooked them too much. I was slow taking the bakery rolls out of the oven and they were charred on top. I kept on thinking how nice this would be if Candy hadn't selected this night to track me to my lair.

80

I didn't feel complimented. I felt like a kid who had looked forward to getting a certain toy on Christmas and gets two other toys, neither of which he wants. That was the way it was. Sure, I wanted Dana. But not this way.

The dinner was not a startling success. Dana and Candy were apparently having a grand time, which only served to irk me more. I contributed my ten cents' worth to the conversation, but what I said didn't rate being written down for posterity. But it was the best I could do under the circumstances. The whole thing was a mess.

Time passed faster than I would have believed possible. I didn't realize that it was almost midnight until Dana got up and reached for her coat. Candy made a similar gesture, but Dana stopped her. She said, "Just because I'm a poor working goil is no reason for you to break your evening off in the middle."

Candy didn't need much persuading. She let herself be talked into staying.

Dana rejected my suggestion that I taxi her back to the club. Both she and Candy went thumbs down on the idea that we all go. I took Dana to the elevator. I said, "I'm awful sorry, honey. This wasn't the way . . ."

She gave me a sugary smile. "We had almost as much privacy as we would have had at the club, didn't we Kirk?"

The elevator door slid open. She stepped into the cage. It dropped out of sight. I said a few profane words and started back into the apartment.

Wonderful evening. Everything just dandy.

Candy was carrying dishes into the kitchen, scraping them and holding them under the hot-water faucet. Maybe she was a screwball, but she was also a pretty good kid. I pitched in with her. There didn't seem to be anything else to do.

She said, "I really loused things up, didn't I?"

I smiled vaguely and didn't say Yes or No.

"Trouble with you," she went on, "is that you've got too much masculine charm, too much personality—"

"And a few brains."

She gave me time to cool down. I didn't know what she was thinking about Dana and me, but whatever it was, I felt sure I wouldn't like it.

81

We got things straightened up. Candy found a bottle of benedictine and poured two thimblefuls. She set them on the coffee table and seated herself on the couch. She produced a platinum cigarette case. She lighted two cigarettes and passed one to me. She patted the cushion alongside her, and I sat on it. She said, "Alone at last."

I thought of an answer to that one, but kept it to myself.

After a while she said, "May I talk?"

"Sure. Go right ahead."

"When I came over here tonight, I had an idea. I've still got it."

"That puts you one up on me."

"Are you interested?"

"Of course . . ." What else could I say?

She started, stopped, and then started again. That was unusual for Miss Candy Livingston. I glanced at her. Her cheeks were flushed.

She said, "I'm asking you a straight question, Kirk. You can give me a straight answer. But more than anything else, I want you to believe I'm serious."

I waited. I thought I was prepared for anything, and I was. For anything except what came next.

"You're a very attractive man, Mr. Douglas," she said slowly. "How would you like to marry twenty million dollars?"

XIII

I DON'T KNOW how I took that one. Instinctively, I knew she wasn't kidding, but even then I couldn't believe it.

Twenty million dollars is a lot of money. Candy Livingston was a lot of girl. The combination was good. It wasn't something you could laugh off even if you understood it. I didn't.

I had gotten along pretty well up to now. I didn't have to fight my way through college. I stepped into a fair job when I graduated, then I had a stretch in the army, and then I had walked into another job. My work seemed to suit Yarborough

& Jensen, and it looked as though I might be going places. But not the places Candy was offering.

I sat on the couch alongside of her, doing nothing and saying the same thing. For the first time in our brief and unusual acquaintanceship, she was embarrassed. She dropped her cigarette in the ash try and let it smoulder. I reached over and ground it out. I could hear traffic noises. I could even hear the whirr inside the electric clock on the mantel.

I wanted to talk, but I couldn't figure what to say. If it were a gag, I didn't want to appear to take it seriously. If she was serious, I was equally anxious not to hurt her feelings. It was a ridiculous position for a man to be in. Especially a man named Kirk Douglas.

She said quietly, "You can't quite figure whether I mean it, can you?"

I nodded.

"I mean it. Straight across the board."

"Why?" The question popped out before I knew I was going to ask it.

She hesitated. "Perhaps," she said, "because I'm in love with you."

Once again I was hanging on the ropes. I didn't know the procedure in a case like this. The faintest sort of a smile showed briefly on her lips. She said, "Unaccustomed as you are to public proposals . . . you still make some sort of an answer."

"All right." I took her hand. "I think you mean it. I still can't figure why, and I still don't believe you'd want me to take you up on it."

"I know what I want. I usually get it."

"That isn't the point, Candy. Let me ask you a question: How many times have you been in love?"

"I lost count long ago."

"You see!"

"I don't see anything." She toyed with the platinum cigarette case. "I wish people could talk about love without being trite. But it isn't possible. There's been so much written about it that you always sound like you're repeating something you've read." She let that sink in, and then went on. "Get this straight, Kirk. I've absorbed a large slice of life in my
83

twenty-two years. That makes me wild, but it doesn't make me dumb. When the real thing comes along: I know it."

There it was. On a solid gold platter, ready to serve. I felt sorry as hell. What she was doing took courage. My knowledge of the English language wasn't helping me. I knew the words, but I didn't have the thoughts to back them up.

She stared at me levelly with her big blue eyes. I said slowly, "I wish we'd met a couple of years ago, Candy."

She nodded. "I thought it was that way."

"Let me explain. Dana and I want to get married. Unfortunately, her husband doesn't see it like that."

She laughed. There wasn't much mirth in it. She said, "Candy Livingston also ran."

"You're a grand pal. It just happens that I'm all tied up emotionally."

She asked abruptly, "How come Ricardo can't be pushed into a divorce?"

I gave it to her briefly. There was an interesting light in her eyes. "I'm not checking out," she said. "Not as long as Dana stays married."

I still couldn't think of anything that fitted. I liked her better, at that moment, than ever before. But that wasn't being in love. She wasn't Dana. She straightened up, and started to laugh. "I've really put you on the spot, haven't I?"

I said, "I'm dazed, that's all."

"I'll answer some of the questions you're too considerate to ask. I fell for you the night I met you. Don't ask me why. I wouldn't be knowing the answer myself. I thought you could be had—in one way or another. I was all full of bright remarks: you would make your passes, and I'd tell you that the line formed on the right. But nothing like that happened, and I found myself staying awake nights thinking about you. The more I thought, the more it seemed to me that I'd enjoy having you around all the time. Maybe it's because you didn't make a play for me."

She reached for another cigarette and lighted it. "Just remember this Kirk: Until you hear from me to the contrary, the proposal stands. Nod your head and I'll come running. Now let's drop it."

That suited me fine. I started to say something. I don't

know what it was, but it didn't matter because I never finished. A pair of arms were around my neck, a pair of soft, warm lips were pressed against mine. The universe commenced spinning.

She pulled away and got up. She said, "Better fix yourself up. You're all over lipstick."

I went into the bathroom and looked in the mirror. I dabbed at my lips. I walked back into the room and tried to be nonchalant. I wouldn't have gotten away with it except that she was willing to string along.

She carried the ball from then on. No more talk of love or marriage. She'd made her pitch and it hadn't worked out. She was more of a person than I had thought. Crazy as three seagulls, perhaps, but there was something solid underneath.

We sat around and talked. We killed a lot of time. We killed it until almost three o'clock.

I insisted on taking her home. I knew she had an estate on Long Island, but that wasn't where I took her. I rode her to a white apartment house that had a lobby choked with chromium and glass. She didn't ask me upstairs. I went back in the same taxi. I flopped in my reading chair and said, "Wow!" I felt uncomfortable and at the same time I felt good. It was something to reflect that I had said No to twenty million dollars.

This was another night when I was slated to stay awake. There were getting to be too many of them. I made some firm resolutions. Early to bed, early to rise, makes a man . . . and I let it stop there.

At four o'clock my eyes were still pinned back. I was thinking of a lot of things and none of them fitted.

I was trying to connect Candy Livingston with the hundred thousand dollars which had been put to my credit at the bank. It wouldn't mean a thing to her, and she might have felt that it would boost my morale when the big moment occurred. But that was wrong, too, because when the hundred thousand had been given to me I hadn't even met Candy. I had no reason to believe she knew I was alive. So what might have been a good theory had to be pitched out of the window.

I don't know what time I got to sleep. I do know that I felt drugged when the alarm clock went off. I took a shower and shaved while the coffee was percolating. I drank three cups of it. I looked out of the window and watched the sun trying to come up. I said, "Aw nuts!" and reached for my coat and hat. I got to the office late. A couple of the boys grinned and winked. They probably thought I had a hangover.

I telephoned Arthur and invited him to have dinner with me that night. At a nice, quiet, little table d'hote restaurant. He said he'd be tickled pink, and told me he was back on full-time duty and feeling good. His arm was sore, but it didn't really bother him.

I held off speaking to Dana until late afternoon. When I did call her to say I wouldn't be seeing her that evening, she was perfect. Her only reference to the previous night was casual. We talked for a few minutes and that was that.

Arthur met me at the restaurant. He looked nervous and worried, but that was nothing new. He asked how my work for Ferguson was getting on. We finished eating and went back to my apartment.

Arthur flopped in one chair and I sprawled out in another. Arthur pulled out a cigarette and tried to fit it into his holder. He used a special kind of a gadget that was supposed to protect him from nicotine. He was afraid of getting stomach ulcers.

The holder dropped out of his hand and rolled under the couch. He got down on his hands and knees and started searching for it. I started to help him, and he said he had it. He got up with the holder, and also with something else. He said, "You should tell the maid to sweep behind the couch, too."

I shrugged. He said, "Finder's keepers, isn't it?"

"It all depends on what you find."

"A quarter." He smiled. "That's a lot of money to a guy like me."

He held it in his palm. I looked at it without interest. Then something clicked. I said, "Let me see that."

He seemed surprised by my abruptness. He handed me the coin.

It was a quarter, all right, but it was like no other quarter in the world. One segment of it, perhaps a fifth of the coin, was absolutely flat. The rest of it was okay. Arthur said, "You can have it. I don't believe it could be spent."

I was staring at the coin. My brain was doing nip-ups.

I said, "You found this under the couch, Arthur?"

"Yeh. Sure. Why?"

I turned it over and looked at the other side. That was flat, too. I don't know what else I expected. Ideas were crowding in on me; ideas that I didn't like.

Arthur said, "Why all the excitement over a bum quarter?"

I said, "This is a very special quarter, Arthur. I know who it belongs to."

"Well . . . ?"

"It belongs to Ricardo. It's his luck piece. He'd rather lose his right eye than this."

Arthur shrugged. "So it's a busted quarter and you found it. You give it back to him. What's wrong with that?"

"More than you know." I moistened my lips. "I'm wondering how it got here. Ricardo has never been in my apartment."

Arthur said, "You're nuts. If the coin was here, Ricardo must have been."

"Not when I was at home."

Arthur and I stared at each other. I knew we must be thinking the same thing. Maybe Ricardo *had* been in my apartment one night when I wasn't at home.

Maybe he had been there with a girl named Ethel Brower.

XIV

A SILVER COIN. A busted quarter that had been stepped on by a streetcar and wasn't worth any part of two bits. A coin that was worth a million in superstition to its owner and which had no business at all in my apartment.

I kept turning it over and over like a pancake that wouldn't cook the same on both sides. I could be wrong, of course. Maybe another streetcar had run over one-fifth of another silver quarter. That was possible, but improbable. What was even more improbable was that the second silver quarter should find its way into my room.

It was a nice room, but too many things had happened in it recently. Too many things that didn't belong. This battered coin, for one thing. The body of a girl who had been strangled to death, for another.

Arthur Maybank sat watching me. He ran slim, delicate fingers through hair that was too sparse for so young a man, and waited for me to say something. He didn't have long to wait.

I said, "You've known Ricardo and Dana almost as long as I have. Didn't either of them ever tell you about this?"

He shook his head. Then he smiled, just a little bit. "And so far," he said, "you haven't either."

"It's quite a story. It deals with superstition, and your scientifically trained mind will reject it. But you musn't."

He said, "I won't. I meet a lot of superstitious people at the hospital."

"The yarn goes back about ten or twelve years. At that time Ricardo Sanchez was unknown. He was a fairly good-looking guy who knew a lot of dancing and wanted to do something about it. All he'd ever succeeded in doing was to remain in a half-starved condition. Like a lot of optimists on the fringe of show business, he wouldn't give up. Maybe he was too lazy to do regular work; maybe he had the soul of an artist. Knowing him, you can take your choice.

"Whatever breaks he'd been having were bad ones. He had extended his limited credit until his friends either cut corners to avoid him or he did the same to them for fear they'd request the return of loans which he couldn't return. He had an agent—they all do—and he had borrowed so much from his agent that he never went near the office. He was ill-fed, poorly clothed, discouraged and just about ready to become a beautiful floorwalker so that he could eat occasionally.

"One day, crossing Third Avenue, he saw something on the car track. It was a quarter. A car had run over a small portion of it. Four-fifths of the coin was still good money. The remaining fifth was flat. What it meant to Ricardo right then was doughnuts and coffee, provided he could persuade someone to take it.

"His version of what happened is rather vivid. He went into a greasy little place called The Coffee Pot. He asked the

88

tough gent behind the counter whether he'd accept the mashed quarter. The counterman told him to get the hell out of there: he didn't have no time to waste on no bums.

"Up to that moment, according to Ricardo, he had reconciled himself to slow starvation. Having been almost in possession of something to eat impelled him to do something he would never otherwise have done. He went looking for the only person he knew who might possibly stand another touch: his agent. He wanted to sell his quarter to the agent for a quarter he could spend. He wanted food."

I paused long enough to fill my pipe and light it. "I'm giving you the details, Arthur, because they're very important. Without them, you'll never understand how a thing like this can come to mean so much to an otherwise intelligent man."

"Don't apologize." Arthur was leaning back and watching me through half-closed eyes. "I'm more than interested."

"Knowing that he faced a two-to-one chance of being pitched out on his ear, Ricardo went to his agent's office. He met the agent just as he stepped inside the door. But to his amazement, he didn't get thrown out. The ten-per-center grabbed him and said Ricardo was just the man he wanted to see. He said there was an immediate opening in the chorus of a new musical that was on the verge of a Broadway opening. Would Ricardo take it? Ricardo would. He did. At the same time he borrowed five dollars from his agent. He didn't say anything about the flattened quarter. He kept that in his pocket and started thinking of it as a luck piece.

"He got the job. He held it. What was more, he studied the routines of the dance team that was featured in the show. One night, in the middle of the show, the male half of the dance team turned his ankle. They were about to cut the spot when Ricardo convinced the stage manager that he could do it. They let him try it. He grabbed twice as much applause as the principal had ever received. When he finished, he felt in his pocket and found the coin had been with him. He didn't need any more convincing. It was a luck piece, all right.

"He kept that coin, and he started up. He was a natural-born dancer, and all he had needed was the opportunity. Before the end of that show's run, he and a girl partner had supplanted the original couple. He and the girl went from there into a nice, small club as a ballroom team. Wham! Then a better engagement and another one still better.

"The rest you know. He became recognized as one of the greatest ballroom dancers in the world. He finally met Dana, saw that she was the answer to a dancer's prayer, taught her all he knew—and married her. And through all of this he held tight to that luck piece. He credited it with all the luck he'd had. Several years ago he bought one of those little flat 18-carat cases which are called pill boxes. He had it lined with purple velvet and he put his luck piece in it. There's probably nothing in the world he values so highly."

I ran out of breath. Arthur said, "If it means that much to him—and if he lost it—why wouldn't he have missed it?"

"Because of the little gold pill box. I imagine that after all these years a man wouldn't be opening it all the time to see whether the luck piece was there. As long as he had the gold box, he'd presume the coin was inside. That could explain why he hasn't missed it."

"Maybe he has."

I shook my head. "I don't think so. I'd have heard about it. So would everybody else who knows him."

Arthur said, "You think that the box might have opened and the coin dropped out . . . under certain circumstances?"

"It's possible. If Ricardo happened to be under enough nervous strain at the time, he might not notice."

"That still doesn't explain why he was here. You say he has never visited you. If you're right on that, he must have been here when you were out." Arthur crossed one leg over the other. "That's rather far-fetched, isn't it, Kirk?"

"Tell me how else could the coin get here?"

"All right. But you may not like it. Suppose Dana brought it."

I gave that a thorough going-over. I said, "I can't buy that one, Arthur. First, she wouldn't dare to take the luck piece out of the box. Second, she would have had no reason for doing it. Third, she wouldn't have brought it here. Fourth, if she had done all this—and had lost it—she would have told me."

He smiled. "You make out a pretty good case. Which leaves us with only one alternative. If it's the same coin, then

Ricardo must have brought it. So let's ask ourselves this: When did he come and why?"

I said, "A girl I never saw in my life—a girl named Ethel Brower—was murdered in this apartment on the third of February. There isn't any logical answer to what she was doing here. We can put her in the category with the coin."

"But why here?"

"You had a theory once," I said slowly, "that Ricardo might actually be in love with Dana; that he might have suspected she was coming here that night, and have been jealous. If that were true, he could have made a mistake, killed this Brower woman believing it was Dana . . . then got out as fast as possible."

Arthur looked steadily at me. He said, "I know I suggested that, Kirk. At the time it sounded reasonable. The way you tell it, I can't believe it."

"Why not?"

"Too many flaws. Mind you, I still don't like Ricardo. I still believe that he could be in love with Dana. But where Ethel Brower fits in or why Ricardo should have met her here . . ."

I said, "We don't know anything about the people Ricardo knew . . . long ago. This Brower woman could have fitted in there, couldn't she?"

"Naturally. But look, Kirk . . . it's still all full of holes."

"Okay. But these things have happened. We didn't imagine them. Not any more than you imagined you were shot at. Where does that belong in this crazy pattern? And what do I do next?"

Arthur said, "If I were you I'd take it to the police."

I hesitated. "I may have to eventually. But not until I'm forced."

"Why?"

"Dana. You understand the situation between Dana and me. But what would the public think?"

"Yeh . . . I know . . ."

"And suppose Ricardo isn't mixed up in all this stuff. I give this coin to the cops and what do they do? They start shoving him around. The newspapers get it. It'd make juicy copy."

"Suppose he *is* the bad boy?"

"The minute I'm convinced of that, I'll tell the police. Up to now, they're as stalled as I am. They know about the killing of Ethel Brower. They know that somebody deposited a hundred thousand dollars to my credit at the bank. They know someone tried to kill you for no discernible reason except that you are a friend of mine—"

"That's ridiculous!"

"Don't kid yourself. That's the only possible motive, even though it doesn't make a nickel's worth of sense. I'm in the middle of something I don't understand. But I can't see myself throwing Ricardo—and, incidentally, Dana—to the wolves without more proof than this."

"Isn't it a bit dangerous, playing detective, Kirk?"

"I'm not playing detective. I don't know anything about that sort of thing. And I'm not withholding evidence. I'm only waiting until I can convince myself that it is evidence."

"I get it . . ." Arthur strolled into the kitchenette and poured himself a glass of water from the little bottle I kept in the icebox. He came back and put it on the coffee table. "What do you do now?" he asked.

"First I'll think things over. Then I'm going to find out for sure whether this actually is Ricardo's luck piece or whether I've run into a coincidence to end all coincidences."

"Which you don't believe."

"Naturally not."

"How will you find out?"

"I'll ask Dana."

"How would she know?"

"She can look in the little gold box. He changes it from one suit to another. Sometimes he leaves it in his street clothes while he's dancing. Sometimes he leaves it on his make-up table. She could go into his dressing room, pick her time and peep inside. If the coin is there, okay. If it isn't, I won't need any further confirmation."

"Of what?" he asked dryly.

"Of the fact that this one belongs to Ricardo."

"And then . . . ?"

"Quit shoving me. I don't know 'what then.' I don't know anything. Maybe I'll turn it over to the police. Maybe I'll get scared of what might happen to Dana in the way of scandal . . . and that'll frighten me off. I'm only sure of one thing: Whatever I do will probably turn out to be wrong."

He said, "Hold it, Kirk. And grab yourself a big night's sleep, starting as of now."

"I'm going to the Caliente."

"Not tonight, you're not. You're bleary-eyed. You'd probably mess things up. Give yourself a day to get adjusted."

I nodded. "You win," I said. "I'll surround myself with sweetness and light. I'll sleep like a baby. Like hell I will."

"Try it anyway," he said. "Maybe you'll be surprised."

I did try it. I crawled into bed and turned out the lights.

Arthur made a good guess. I slept soundly until the alarm clock went off at 7:30.

I didn't feel good. That would have been asking too much. But I did feel better. "By tomorrow morning," I told myself, "I should know a lot more than I know now."

I was right.

XV

THE NEXT day started off fine. I was bent over my drawing board when a secretary appeared at my elbow and said Mr. Jensen wanted to see me. I slicked my hair down, loosened my tie so I'd look as though I'd been working twice as hard, and followed the girl.

Mr. Jensen was at his desk. My office building sketches were scattered all around. For preliminary stuff, it was fairly neat, but Jensen was too smart a cookie to be fooled by pretty sketches. He hadn't got where he was by anything less than solid architectural brains.

He motioned me to a seat. He picked up one sketch in each hand and smiled.

"Nice," he said. "You've got ideas, Douglas."

I flushed all over. Tell me I'm pretty and I'll call you a liar. But say something nice about my professional ability and I'll blush like a schoolgirl.

He put the sketches back down on the desk. He said,

"Maybe Ferguson will like them—maybe he won't. I thought it only fair to let you know that Yarborough and I think you've got something. We can always find a client who would be interested in this sort of work."

He smiled again, started attending to something else. I took the hint. I said, "Thanks, Mr. Jensen," and floated out of the room. What he had done made me realize that from now on I rated with Yarborough & Jensen. I was something more than just another guy who could make marks with drawing instruments.

Jensen's praise was like a shot in the arm. I labored like a fiend. My aching backbone reminded me that the working day had ended. I washed up, telephoned Dana, and dropped in at her apartment. One look at her and I forgot what I had come for. I started doing affectionate things, and she acted as though she liked them. I bubbled over like a kid, telling her about Jensen. She seemed to be fascinated. She said, "You watch me dance, Kirk—and you've got a certain light in your eyes: I hear about your work, and feel the same way about you. Maybe we're pretty proud of each other."

I sat on the couch and she mixed me a short one. I fished into my pocket and took out a shiny bit of metal. I showed it to her. I said, "Did you ever see that before?"

Her eyes got wide. "Of course. That's Ricardo's luck piece. Where did you get it?"

"I'll explain later. Meanwhile, are you sure"

She took it and turned it over and over. Then she handed it back. "Sure I'm sure. There couldn't be two like it."

"Suppose I put the edge of a quarter on the streetcar track and waited until a car passed. Just to be cute. I'd have one that looked just like this, wouldn't I?"

"Yes . . . But it wouldn't make a lot of sense." She was frowning. I loved her frown. Her nose crinkled up when she did it. She said, "It *is* Ricardo's, isn't it?"

"That's what I want to find out."

I was staring at the quarter. It held a lot of interest for me. I spoke again without looking at her.

"Has Ricardo said anything about missing it?"

"No."

"Would he if he had?"

94

She laughed. "You frame your sentences beautifully, darling. The answer is that if he had, he most certainly would."

I took her hand. "Could you find out, Dana?"

"Yes. He hasn't carried it when he was dancing since one night in Chicago when it fell out on the floor and he ruined the number by stopping to retrieve it. When he's on, it either stays in his street clothes or, if he plans to shift into another suit, he leaves it on his make-up table."

I said, "There's no rush about this. I'd like you to look inside that box sometime when he doesn't know you're doing it. If it has disappeared, and he doesn't know—I'd be just as happy if he didn't find out."

"Want me to put it back?"

"No-o. Not yet."

Dana said, "You're being mysterious. Why the secrecy?"

"I don't want to make statements until I'm more sure than I am now."

"You win." She got up, letting her hand rest on my shoulder. She said, "What's the program for tonight?"

"Usual thing. I'm no longer the exhausted man. I think we should drink Mr. Jensen's health. We might also toast Ferguson for rescuing me from the architectural doldrums. We can do all that with dinner—between shows."

She vanished into the bedroom. I picked up a magazine and riffled through the pages. I didn't bother reading. My head was too full of pleasant thoughts. This looked like my day. I was loving it.

Ricardo was at the club when we got there. He already had changed from street clothes to white tie and tails. Dana gave me a significant look. She started back for the dressing room corridor and I went to my pet table. Ricardo walked across to the bandstand and talked to the leader. They both started making rhythmic motions with their right hands, so I fancied they were discussing tempo. The next time I looked, Ricardo had disappeared.

The chorus girls started grouping near me, waiting for the opening number. One or two of them spoke to me, and then the big spot went on, the music swelled and they were off: gay, artificial smiles on hard, youthful faces.

The show went off as usual. Everything timed to the minute. A few seconds before Dana & Ricardo were due on, they appeared in the opening between the club and the corridor.

They were quarreling bitterly. Their faces were like thunderclouds. Ricardo had hold of Dana's arm, and his grip wasn't gentle. He was talking fast, and I was glad I wasn't a lip reader because I had a hunch I'd resent what he was saying.

Dana wasn't just taking it. Whatever it was about, she was giving as good as she got. It wasn't a pretty picture.

The emcee teed off on their introduction. Ricardo raced to the other side of the bandstand. Dana passed my table without even looking at me. Then came their music cue, and they were on the floor.

The transformation was magical. All traces of anger had vanished. They were smiling at each other. Ricardo swept her into his arms and they flowed into an exquisite tango. They went through their three numbers and did two encores. They took their bows hand in hand and finally they were through. When they passed me, their faces were again contorted with anger, and their words—whatever they were saying—were bitter.

I didn't like any part of it, but it was wonderful. All dance teams quarrel, especially just after they've come off the floor. It's a logical and natural reaction from nervous tension. But this was different. I waited.

I didn't wait long. Dana showed up, dressed for the street. She paused long enough to say, "Let's go," and I trailed her toward the lobby. Somebody called to her, and she waved at them, but she couldn't quite get around to smiling. She was tight as a fiddle string.

We pushed through the revolving door and she said, "Let's walk." I fell into step and she headed toward the park. She walked fast, and didn't talk. Neither did I.

We entered the park at Fifth Avenue and Fifty-ninth Street. We walked down a little hill and past the lake where swans float around in summer and people skate in winter. Nobody was skating now. A thaw was on and the red ball was down.

The patches of snow were ghostly. The trees were bare and disconsolate. The whole place looked forgotten. A car whizzed past occasionally as though in a hurry to get out. Dana continued to walk, and continued to say nothing.

We skirted the zoo and walked all the way to the Mall before she spoke. Then she said something, and her voice was sharp as a razor's edge. She said, "Ricardo's luck piece has disappeared."

I had thought it was something like that. It confirmed certain ideas, but it made me worry more about other things. I said, "He caught you looking?"

"Yes. I figured I had time. I went into his dressing room and opened the box. He came in and snatched it from me."

"Snatched?"

"Yes. His remarks from then on came straight out of the gutter."

I squeezed her arm. I had some foolish idea that it might help. I said, "Did he seem surprised to find the box empty?"

"I don't know . . ." She appeared to be puzzled. "I don't know whether he was surprised, or whether he was furious because I had discovered it."

That was an angle. I asked, "What did he actually say?"

"He accused me of stealing the coin. He demanded that I return it. He said I'd hidden it somewhere, and that he'd rip every stitch of clothes off me to find it."

"Was it an act, Dana—or was he serious?"

"It could have been either. Now will you tell me where you found it?"

"I found it in my apartment. It was evidently caught between the carpet and the wall. My guess is that it had been there a long time."

She stopped walking. Then she shook her head. "That isn't possible," she said. "He's never been in your apartment."

There was only one answer to that. She and I went deep into a discussion which was almost a repetition of the talk I'd had with Dr. Arthur Maybank the previous night. Dana said, "Of course, Ricardo knew a lot of people before I met him. But he never mentioned anybody named Ethel Brower."

I didn't tell her what Arthur had suggested: that Ricardo might have killed Ethel Brower in the mistaken belief that he was strangling Dana.

We kept on walking. It was too cold to do anything else.

We were near the reservoir before she spoke again. She said, "Things can't go on this way, Kirk."

I wrapped my fingers around her arm. I stopped walking. I said, "Get a grip on yourself, honey. You're upset. You're angry with Ricardo. You're worried."

She was standing close. The still, cold air was all around us; the park lights cast weird shadows on the snow. Dana was trembling. I put my arms around her. For a moment she stayed that way, her body rigid. Then it melted. Her arms circled my neck. Her voice wasn't hard any more; it was the shaken voice of a woman who had been asked to bear more than was possible.

She said, "Don't you see why we can't keep this up, Kirk? It's not what happened tonight. It's what happens every night. Tonight only made me see things more clearly. It gave me more courage."

I brushed my lips against her forehead. "Courage for what?"

"Courage to suggest what I've wanted to say for a long time." Her voice got tiny and frightened. "I'm not free, darling. If I wait for Ricardo, I'll never be free. Not ever." She drew back in my arms and looked up at me. "Don't make it too difficult for me, Kirk. Surely you understand what I'm trying to say."

I shook my head. "What is it, Dana?"

Her eyes did not waver. She said, "It isn't fair for us to be separated, Kirk. It isn't fair to either of us."

I said, "Hush . . ." as though I were talking to a child. But she didn't hush.

"We mustn't let ourselves be cheated out of the thing that means most to both of us, darling. And there's only one answer. I want to come and live with you."

XVI

HER WORDS hit me right where I lived. I let them sink in and wondered what to say.

It wasn't easy. I thought of a lot of things, but each sounded more trite than the last. All were inadequate. They had been said before by other men under other circumstances. For that reason, they'd be bound to sound corny.

We stood there looking at each other. She was waiting for me to say something and I wasn't saying it. I did the next best thing. I put my arms around her again. If a sparrow cop had come along, we'd have looked very silly: a man and a girl locked tight in the middle of some very cold winter.

Then I said things. They were the things a kid might say to his first girl—and they were said that way. I wanted Dana to understand how much I loved her; how deeply I was touched by what she was offering. It was important for her to understand that because I knew I was going to turn it down.

I released her, then took her arm and started walking. She walked, too. You could hear our thoughts racing.

Inside, I was all mixed up. Emotions and common sense were having themselves a pitched battle. It would have been easy and delightful to say Yes. But I knew I was going to say No. Only trouble was, I didn't know how to do it. The situation was delicate. I could turn her down and feel noble. But I didn't want to feel noble. I didn't care how I felt. It was Dana I was concerned about.

I said, "Let's keep one thing in mind, sweetheart. I love you."

That wasn't too good, but it wasn't too bad, either. I had said it before, but it still fitted. She didn't even look at me. I hadn't covered quite enough territory. I tried again.

"The idea is startling. It's the thing I'd like second best in the world."

"And the first best?"

"Would be to marry you."

"We're back where we started," she said.

I asked, "Shall I diagram it?"

"That's what I've been waiting for."

"All right. The words are going to be all mixed up. They're going to sound cold and logical instead of the way I want them to sound. They're going to make me out a wooden Indian."

"In other words . . ." She took the play away from me, "You're refusing."

99

I tightened my fingers on her arm. It was the most precious arm in the world. The girl it belonged to was the most precious girl. I said, "Let's don't put it in simple words, Dana. It isn't a simple matter. It's merely that I'm looking farther ahead than you are."

"That's our trouble," she retorted with some bitterness. "We've always looked so far ahead that we've failed to understand what's happening right now. And don't tell me that I'm acting on impulse. Don't tell me that I'm angry with Ricardo. Quarreling with him tonight only served to crystallize ideas I've had for a long time."

I said, "It wouldn't work out. You're not the sort of girl who could live with a man she wasn't married to and get away with it."

"I'm not afraid of what people would say."

"It isn't people I'm afraid of. It's you. There would always be that between us. You'd always be wondering what I was thinking."

"Doesn't that seem rather unimportant, Kirk?"

"No." I stopped walking and so did she. "I'm going to quit sparring," I said. "I'll hand it to you straight, and you'll either understand it or you won't. You want this maybe a tenth as much as I do. You're the one who would be sacrificing something. It's a sacrifice I won't let you make."

"I've thought it over."

"Then you've thought the wrong way. You've probably tried to justify and rationalize a move which you instinctively know is wrong. Oh! I'm not talking morals. What you're suggesting wouldn't be immoral—no matter what people might think. It wouldn't be immoral, but it would be wrong because it would be foolish. You've *got* to see what I'm driving at! Get it into your pretty head that I'm not a prude. It all adds up to this: What we both want is permanence. We wouldn't get it that way."

"What does that make me?"

"The sweetest, bravest girl I've ever known. And if you start feeling sorry for what you've done, I'll pin your ears back."

Her eyes held mine. They were fine, steady eyes. They saw in my face a lot of things I hadn't been able to put into words.

Then, for the first time, a little smile played about her lips. She said, "You're right, Kirk. I was afraid you would be."

"Afraid?"

"I wanted you to do the wrong thing. I wanted you to say Yes. I wanted you to be swept by your desire for me . . ."

"That," I said, "would be easy."

"But it won't happen. I know. As a matter of fact, I agree with you." She laughed. "My God!" she said, "the tricks that intelligence can play!"

We started walking again, this time toward Fifth Avenue. I said, "Is it necessary for me to start building up again to make you understand how much this has meant to me?"

"You know better than that, darling. And I don't feel like a woman scorned. I don't feel that you have rejected me. I don't feel anything but grateful—and disappointed."

We looked at each other and smiled. "Okay now?" I asked.

"Okay, Mister."

And it was okay. That was Dana. No putting me on the spot. Instead of driving us farther apart, this had drawn us closer. She said, "If you ever change your mind, Kirk—I can be had." She said it lightly, with an obvious effort to relieve the tension.

I said, "I'll come up and see you sometime."

We left the park and walked as far as Lexington. We went into a hamburger stand and sat on red leather stools in front of a polished white counter. We ordered hamburgers and steaming coffee. Until we started to eat, we didn't realize that we'd forgotten dinner altogether.

The place was immaculate. We were the only customers. The counterman looked us over and walked to the front of his place where he stood staring moodily out into the street. Everything was back to normal again.

Dana smiled at me without turning her head. She smiled into the big polished mirror and I smiled back the same way. She said, "I should feel embarrassed."

"*You* should? What about me?"

"You're a big strong man. You've done your good deed for the day."

"And in consequence, I feel like a dope."

"That's nice, she said. "I hoped you would."

We wound up with more coffee and some sugared doughnuts. We were beginning to get down to earth. Dana said, "At least I won't hate myself in the morning."

"I wish I could say the same thing."

"Pure," she said, touching my cheek. "Pure as the driven snow."

"You could have gone on," I grinned. "You could have said, 'and twice as cold'."

We were back in the groove by the time we finished our informal meal. We stopped at the cash register and paid the counterman. I left a tip that made his eyes bug out. He said, "Good luck, buddy," and I thought I knew what he meant. I looked at Dana and she giggled. Then I knew that everything was right as rain.

The Caliente was jammed when we got there. Chris, the doorman, greeted us. The head waiter walked around the velvet rope and said, "Somebody been asking for you two."

"Who?"

"Candy Livingston. She's got a big party tonight." He gave a little thought to his next comment, and then took a chance. "She's kinda high," he said.

It was a gay party, all right: a long table at the ringside. Candy was there, looking as though she'd been poured into the black evening gown which set off her blonde beauty to rare advantage. She was surrounded by a half dozen other people. Across the table from Candy sat Agnes Sheridan. Arthur Maybank wasn't anywhere around, but that didn't surprise me because this was one of his duty nights at the hospital.

Candy saw us coming. As an interceptor, she was good. She said to Dana, "I've already got three extra places at the table. That hooks Kirk as of now, and you and Ricardo later."

They talked for a few seconds, and then Dana rushed off to dress for the supper show. Candy dragged me after her and introduced me all around. She sat me next to her, which put me right across from Agnes.

I was interested in Agnes. She seemed to have plenty on the ball, and I wondered what she saw in Arthur. Maybe, I reflected, it was that he was a doctor in the hospital where she was a lowly nurse's aide, so that she saw something other than the puny frame and shy manner of a little man who was considerably less than a shining personality socially. But looking her over now, she seemed to me to belong more definitely with Candy Livingston than with Arthur. And Candy seemed to think so, too. I gathered from snatches of conversation that Miss Livingston and Miss Sheridan had been seeing quite a bit of each other.

Candy's party was in high gear when I sat down. The hostess was particularly gay. Once she leaned over and whispered, "Changed your mind yet, Big Boy?"

I laughed and pretended not to take her seriously. She said, "Are you hard to get!" and the scene in the park flashed back to me. It all made me feel slightly ridiculous.

The show started and finished. A few minutes later Dana joined our table and right behind her came Ricardo. They paid no attention to each other, and I didn't know whether the fight was continuing.

Ricardo was still working on Candy. But he was overdoing it. Candy winked at me. I had an idea that Ricardo wasn't ever going to get to first base. But he kept right on trying.

I danced with Dana, and asked about Ricardo. She said, "He's still in an ugly mood. But I kept my mouth shut."

"Smart girl."

She glanced at the table. "Candy and Agnes seem to be hitting it off, don't they?"

"I was thinking the same thing. But why not?"

"No reason. As a matter of fact, I like Agnes myself. She'd be good for Arthur."

I said, "How about Candy? Who would she be good for?"

Dana didn't answer immediately. Then she said, "I don't know. Maybe Ricardo. Maybe you."

"We don't play in the same league."

"It could be arranged."

"You flatter me."

"I've flattered you twice tonight. You should be a bundle of conceit."

The party kept going until three o'clock. Candy wanted to continue celebrating. Dana and I talked our way out of it. Ricardo checked in with her suggestion. He was full of optimism.

103

I left Dana in front of her apartment house. I went home and prepared for bed. I set the alarm clock, and knew I wasn't going to like it when it exploded in my ear four hours from now.

I got a glimpse of myself in the bathroom mirror. I didn't think I merited any applause, which was why the night seemed so fantastic.

I thought back beyond that. Within the past week, I had turned down a very gorgeous young lady who offered herself and twenty million dollars. Tonight I had said No to the girl I was in love with.

"If you heard that about someone else," I remarked to my reflection, "you'd say he was a double damn fool."

I snapped out the light, opened the window and slipped into bed. "And," I finished, "you'd be right."

XVII

DURING THE next seventy-two hours I thought of a new invention. It was going to be some sort of a gadget with which you could stop thinking about things you didn't want to think about. With it, I'd be able to concentrate on nice things like Dana Warren and the work I was doing for John Ferguson; and forget all the things that were worrying me. I'd forget—at least temporarily—the girl who had been murdered in my apartment, the hundred thousand dollars, the unknown person who had tried to kill Arthur Maybank, about how Ricardo's luck piece got into my room, and I'd quit wondering why I had become so irresistible.

It was the last item that seemed to stick with me. I checked Dana out. She was foolish enough to be in love with me, and that was swell. But the Candy Livingston set-up still had me buffaloed.

I'm a long way from a prize package. If my face had to be my fortune, I'd owe somebody thirteen cents. I didn't scintillate socially. I was fairly big and rather strong, but nothing to get excited about. I could do the average things in the average way, and when you had said that, you had said it all.

My life had been an open book which anyone was privileged to read—but wouldn't, because it wasn't interesting. Yet suddenly things had started happening all around me. They happened to friends and acquaintances who apparently had committed no sin except to be friends and acquaintances. I wanted somebody to tell me I was figuring wrong. But nobody did; not even Dana.

As a matter of fact, Dana wasn't having any easy time of it herself. She tried not to unload her troubles on me, but there were certain things I couldn't miss. Mostly Ricardo.

According to Dana, he continued to be in a vicious mood. I could understand that a superstitious man might let himself be upset by the loss of a luck piece, but this seemed to be more than that. I still had the battered quarter, and I was keeping it until I decided what to do—or until something else turned up which would justify handing it over to the police.

I wasn't holding out on the cops. I've got a high opinion of the New York police force. They're trained to their jobs and they do 'em well. But they're human. If the coin really meant something, they were welcome to it. If it didn't, I wasn't keen about touching off a scandal in which Dana would be the object of prime interest.

I saw as much of Dana as my work permitted. I made my visits to the club as brief as possible. One reason for that was that I didn't like the change in Ricardo's manner toward me.

He had always ridden me. Now he wasn't doing that. He seldom spoke to me. But he looked at me a lot and there was a light in his eyes I didn't relish. I was developing a beautiful case of the jitters.

Thursday afternoon I got a call from Dana. She phoned to tell me that she wouldn't be home when I got off from work. Ricardo wanted her to rehearse a new routine. She suggested that I pick her up at the rehearsal hall about 5:30. I asked whether it was anything special and she said it was nothing more special than wanting to see me.

I was there at 5:20. The rehearsal hall was an old, barren building in the Fifties. What it had been originally, I haven't the faintest idea. Now, it was a four-story, red-brick building with dingy hallways connected by dark, narrow stairways.

105

There was a room on the second floor which crouched behind a sign reading "Office—Enter."

It was a favorite building for people in show business. It contained a great number of fairly large rooms which had hardwood floors. Each of the rooms also had a small electric phonograph. The din in the hallways was terrific: recorded music blaring, tap dancers tapping, singers singing. I went up to the third floor and walked the length of the hallway toward the big front room where Ricardo & Dana always rehearsed. The door was open. There was a rickety chair in the hall and I parked myself on it. I didn't go into the rehearsal room for two reasons. The first was that I was just as happy to avoid Ricardo. The second reason was that he and Dana were quarreling.

Ricardo was wearing dancing slippers, a pair of old gray slacks and a sport shirt open at the neck. His hair was disheveled and his face covered with perspiration.

Dana looked as cute as a black-and-white kitten. She had on dancing shoes, a white blouse, and black shorts which ended above the knee. She had beautiful legs: smooth and well-shaped. There was a bit of pink ribbon tied around her hair, which was probably what made me think of the kitten.

Rehearsal time is always bad with a dance team. They're ironing out new routines. They're doing things they've never done in public and which haven't yet been grooved. They're tense and nervous. They try lifts and spins which might work and might not.

Ricardo & Dana had a collection of special records. These were pressings made for them from their own orchestrations. One of the records—a very fancy waltz—was playing now. They were dancing, but they didn't look like they looked at the Caliente. They looked like two people in a gymnasium.

They floated past the doorway. Then Ricardo grabbed her and swung her over his head. He spun her around, then twirled her body and let it fall. He caught her just before she hit the floor and started spinning with her again. Dana said, "Oh!" as though something hurt. She jerked away from him, and said, "That's no good."

He growled something which I didn't understand, and she went on: "It just won't work."

106

He walked across to the phonograph and set the needle back. He said, "We'll try it again."

"No. You hurt me."

"So what?"

"I'm not having any more. The whole routine is absurd. It isn't even pretty."

"You're telling me what's good, huh?"

"I'm only saying that part of it is out."

"Oh, yeah . . ." The music had caught up with them. He put his right arm around her and started the lift. She squirmed and pulled away. He staggered back and would have fallen if he hadn't crashed into the wall. He called her a name that could not have offended a female canine, but which sounded harsh and ugly when applied to Dana. I felt my face flushing and my body getting tight. I relaxed with an effort. I said, "Hold on, Kirk—hold on. This is their business."

They started having it out verbally. It wasn't new to me. I had seen other dance teams rehearsing: topflight teams . . . nice people who were turtledoves outside. They all quarreled and argued.

But it didn't take me long to realize that this was different. Ricardo was nasty. He wasn't the suave Ricardo of the Club Caliente. He was Ricky Sanchez of Red Hook.

Once more he dropped the needle where he wanted it. He grabbed her again, and again she tore away from him.

He said something vile. His open hand whipped out. It caught her on the cheek. Hard.

I was in the room before I knew what was happening. This wasn't their business any more. It was mine. Ricardo whirled to face me. He was on his toes, and his face was contorted with anger.

He knew why I was there. He knew it even better than I did. I closed in on him and my fist flashed out. It had everything I could give it. It caught him on the side of the jaw.

He brought up against the table that held the little phonograph. The music kept right on playing. I knew I had started something, but that was the way I had wanted it for a long time.

He smiled. It was a thin, cruel smile. He said, "You've been asking for this, Fauntleroy. Now you're gonna get it."

He slid forward like a boxer. I was ready. Or at least I thought I was. I led with my left and then threw a hard right. He stepped inside of it neatly. His counter—a hard right cross—caught me on the cheek. It calmed me down and told me that I was up against a man who knew his stuff.

He snapped one at my stomach. I blocked that and let fly with my right. Too high. It rolled off his forehead. It couldn't have hurt much.

He was a little larger than I was. I was the better boxer, but this wasn't a boxing match. It wasn't something that could be staged in Madison Square Garden.

It was ugly. Rules were forgotten. Down the hall a woman screamed. Doors opened and the other rehearsal halls disgorged people in odd attires. But I wasn't interested. I had plenty on my hands. More, perhaps, than I could cope with.

Dana was standing against the wall. She hadn't moved. She hadn't said anything.

Ricardo butted me. He brought his right knee up hard against my groin. I returned the compliment. If that was the way he wanted to play, it was okay with me.

There was a commotion in the hall. A husky voice said, "Break it up!" and I saw a blue uniform. There was a silver shield on the blue coat. Behind the cop was a little man I'd never seen before, but who apparently managed the building. He was jumping around and making futile gestures.

The patrolman hauled us to our feet. Ricardo slugged me. It was a Sunday punch and I reeled back from the impact. I started toward him, but I didn't get there. The cop knew his stuff, too. He crowded Ricardo against the wall, holding him with his body. He said, "Quit playin' rough, sonny. Or you're gonna get it how you won't like it."

Ricardo tried to shove past him. Two well-muscled young men who had been rehearsing an adagio act appointed themselves deputies. Each one grabbed an arm. They held Ricardo tight.

Somebody said something to the patrolman. He looked at Ricardo. "You oughta be ashamed," he said. "You're big enough to know better."

Ricardo called him a dirty name. The cop's eyes clouded.

"That'll be enough," he snapped. "By rights I oughta run you in. But if you act nice, I'll lay off. Take it or leave it."

He stepped back. The adagio boys dropped Ricardo's arms. Ricardo looked like a mess. I had a hunch that I looked twice as bad. He said to me in a flat, toneless voice, "This isn't finished, Douglas."

He walked over to the corner where there was a little washstand with running water. He bathed his face and dried it in a towel. He brushed his hair with his hands. He put on his coat and then his overcoat. He clapped his hat on his head and walked out through the buzzing spectators.

I used the basin, too. I washed off some blood. The cold water stung, but it felt good, too. I was beginning to think connectedly again. I hated what had happened.

Dana said, "I'll be back." She went out of the room. The cop looked me over. "Just a private scrap, huh?"

I nodded.

"I wisht I didn't have to break it up," he said. "You was goin' good: the both of you."

Dana came back. She had on a dress, a coat and a hat. She had on street shoes and carried a little bag. She said to the policeman, "May we go?"

"Go ahead." A broad grin split his countenance. "I ain't seen a thing."

Dana and I walked downstairs. We hailed a cab and got in. I gave the address of her apartment.

After a long while, she spoke.

She said, "It wasn't your fault, Kirk. But I'm sorry."

"So am I."

She put an icy hand in mine. "I'm afraid," she said.

I didn't say anything. There was no point to telling her that I was afraid, too.

XVIII

WHEN I shaved the next morning I had lots of no fun. My lower lip was cut inside and puffed outside. There was a bruise on my jaw. I had a bit of a mouse under my left eye, but that didn't interfere with the shaving.

The somewhat ancient and bowlegged doorman took one look at me and grinned. Two girls in the crosstown bus stared and giggled. I hunched my shoulders so they'd look square and stuck my chest out. Maybe they'd think I had fought the main bout in the Garden the previous night.

At the office, the lads in the drafting room gave me a double take. One of them said, "You shouldn't run into doors, Kirk."

I said, "I didn't run into a door. I had a fight, and I didn't do very well."

That puzzled them. If I'd said I had run into a door, they'd think I'd been in a fight. Now that I said I'd been in a fight, the door theory was something for them to chew on. I took off my coat, put on an eyeshade, arranged things on my drawing board and started to work.

Friday and Saturday I stayed away from the Caliente. I saw Dana once and talked to her on the phone several times. I suggested that inasmuch as I looked battered and Ricardo wasn't entirely without scars, it would be better for people not to see us together. I wasn't keen about advertising the fact that Ricardo and I had tangled.

Sunday morning I looked myself over. My appearance was practically normal. I decided to go to the club and have dinner there with Dana. Staying away too long wasn't good, either. I was curious to see Ricardo, also. Not what he looked like, but what his attitude would be.

I waited until early afternoon and telephoned Arthur Maybank at the hospital. His voice sounded sleepy. I invited him to have dinner with me at the Caliente. He said he'd love to, but couldn't. He said he had a date with Agnes Sheridan.

"So bring her with you. We'll watch the show and then Dana will eat dinner with us."

He said, "That sounds fine, but . . . well, let's be honest. I can't afford places like that."

"Be yourself, Arthur. I'm inviting you and Agnes to be my guests. You and she can check out after dinner if you decide you want to be alone."

His voice brightened. He said he'd be at the club with Agnes between 7:15 and 7:30. "It'll be fun," he said. "I'm off duty tonight, with nothing to worry about."

I left home early. The temperature had dropped again. It

was about eighteen. I had time to kill so I dropped into a newsreel theater. I did more thinking than watching.

I had used the last three nights to catch up on lost sleep. I was glad to fall into the groove again at the Caliente. In one way I didn't like the place because every time I saw Dana on the floor it made me feel like excess baggage. But in another way it had become a habit, and habits are hard to break. I hoped Candy wouldn't be there.

I was having a Martini at the bar when Arthur walked in with Agnes. They joined me in a drink, and we were spearing olives when Dana arrived. We went back to my pet table and made ourselves comfortable.

Arthur was cold. He complained that Agnes had walked him through Central Park and that she had made him stand on the shore of the lake and watch people skate.

Dana looked up with interest. "Do you skate, Agnes?"

The dark head nodded. "I love it. But I don't get much chance."

"Where do you go? The park?"

"No. I prefer rinks. I'm not too good at it . . ." The way she said it, I could tell that she was a wow. No Sonja Henie, maybe, but no dub, either.

Agnes said, "I haven't skated once this year."

"You did an awful lot of watching this afternoon," grumbled Arthur.

"That made me hungry for it." She beamed across at Dana. "Why don't we go skating some night?"

"All right, you tell me. Why don't we?"

I had never seen Agnes so eager. She said, "We could slip out right after the dinner show and go to the rink. We'd get a full hour and a half and be back in time for you to dress again."

Dana said, "I'd like that."

"Tomorrow night?"

"Monday . . . ?" Dana nodded. "Perfect! I'll bet you're one of those experts who owns his own skates."

"Yes. That is, I'm not an expert, but I prefer my own skates."

"Bring them with you when you come to dinner. We'll put them in my dressing room. After the dinner show we'll

111

go back there while I change, and then we'll slip out through the other exit."

Agnes turned to Arthur. "How about joining us?"

Arthur's expression was ludicrous. "Me skate? Lady, you don't know whereof you speak. I got on ice skates once in my life. I stayed on them for approximately two seconds. Then I swapped ends. I swore off for life."

She said, "I'll teach you."

"You can teach me a lot of things, Agnes . . . but skating isn't one of them. And it's out on another count. I'm on duty tomorrow night."

"Couldn't you arrange . . . ?"

"Not a chance, even if I wanted to. And I don't."

Agnes invited me. I grinned and said Yes. "I'll spend half the time on my ear," I said, "but I've got the soul of a clown."

"We won't eat anything here," said Agnes. "There's a nice lunch counter at the rink where we can get sandwiches and coffee and pie."

Dana looked at her watch, said, "Oh dear!" and was off like a shot. I didn't see her again until she and Ricardo swept onto the dance floor.

I took a good look at Ricardo. Even allowing for the camouflage which make-up could provide, he didn't show a bruise. I was a little disappointed. I had hit him plenty, and I preferred to believe that when I hit 'em, they stayed hit.

Dana rejoined us after the show. As soon as we finished, I shooed Arthur and Agnes out. I knew that was what they both wanted. Dana watched them until they reached the checkroom. She said, "They've got it bad, haven't they?"

There was the usual buzz of dinner checks being paid before the 10:30 cover charge went on. During all of it, Dana sat quietly. I knew she had something on her mind, and that she'd tell it when she got ready. I didn't have long to wait.

She leaned across the table and touched my hand. Just a touch. She said, "I've got news for you, Kirk."

"Good news?"

"I hope you think so." She reached for one of my cigarettes and I held the match for her. She said, "I'm quitting the act."

It didn't register right away. Then I frowned. "You're *what?*"

112

"I'm quitting. I told Ricardo yesterday that I'd give him a reasonable time, but no more, to find himself another partner."

"Divorce?" I asked eagerly.

"No. As a matter of fact, Ricardo says if I throw him down like this, he'll never give me one."

"Then why . . . ?"

"I've been spineless, Kirk. I've been reaching for the thing I wanted most without being willing to let go of the thing I had. Ricardo has been stalling. I don't mean anything to him as a woman, but I'm egoist enough to believe that I rate pretty high as a dance partner. He wasn't even looking for anybody else. He thought I'd let things rock along."

I said, "There are two sides to that Dana. Dancing means a lot to you. Being half of one of the world's best dance teams is important."

"There's something else that means more."

"I wish we were alone," I said. "I'd like to kiss you."

She smiled. "I know Ricardo. He's hopping mad. He thinks I'm an ingrate and a fool. Even yet he doesn't quite believe me. He won't believe me until I actually leave. Then he'll lose interest in me. He'll find another partner. And he'd have no reason then for not giving me a divorce."

I said, "Has it ever occurred to you, sweetheart—that he may have another reason?"

"What sort of reason?"

"He could be in love with you."

"You suggested that once before. But he isn't. He's in love with himself and with his profession."

"That isn't the way he's acted. He's impressionable. Yet as far as we know, there's been no other woman in his life."

"How about Candy Livingston?"

"Twenty million dollars," I said. "There's your answer." I traced a pattern on the tablecloth with my fingernail. I said, "I'm not sure you've done the right thing."

"That's why I didn't discuss it with you in advance, Kirk. The way things were, I couldn't see anything but a future that offered nothing. This way, there is at least a chance."

"What will you do?"

"I'll get another partner, too. That won't be difficult. He won't be as good as Ricardo. But I'll find one."

I looked at her steadily. "Does Ricardo associate your decision with our battle royal the other afternoon?"

"Probably."

"Has he made any further mention of his lost luck piece?"

She frowned. "Yes. He's superstitious enough to believe that it ties in with my decision to quit."

"Does he know why you were looking for it?"

"No. He asked, of course. I merely told him that I saw the box on his make-up table and opened it. He doesn't believe me, but he can't prove different, either."

I said, "He has lost his luck piece and his dance partner. I wouldn't blame him for being upset."

Dana said, "You haven't told me that you're glad." ·

"I don't know what to tell you, darling. I'm glad and I'm worried. I'm glad because I agree with you that so long as you stayed with Ricardo our problem wouldn't ever be solved. I'm worried . . ."

"You're worried about what?"

I didn't dare to tell her what I was worried about. What good would it do for her to know that Arthur believed that Ricardo had killed Ethel Brower in the dark believing her to be Dana. Arthur might be wrong.

"Skip it," I said. "The important point is that I feel closer to you already. And I love you more than ever."

She reached for my hand. Her eyes were soft and lovely.

"That," she said, "is what I've been waiting to hear."

XIX

Monday afternoon Dana telephoned me at the office. She reminded me that the skating party was still on for that night, said that she still loved me and asked whether I'd drop by her apartment when I knocked off. I said I would and hoped she wouldn't laugh too much when I started punching holes in the ice with my face.

I left the office on the dot and got to her apartment in nothing flat. She opened the door for me, let me kiss her, handed me a long, tall, cool drink and told me to make myself

114

comfortable. She said she had something to show me. I said, "Are you telling me!" and it rolled off her like a duck. I told her she was supposed to laugh at my funny cracks, and all she did was to push me down on the sofa and shove a magazine in the hand that wasn't holding the drink.

She looked beautiful and happy. She moved the bridge lamp to the doorway which connected the living room and bedroom, turned it on full and placed it carefully. Then she went into the bedroom and closed the door, leaving me alone with a lot of nice ideas.

I looked at drawings of pretty ladies in the magazine. My interest in them was entirely clinical. I wondered what was going on in the other room. I didn't wonder very long, because suddenly the door opened and Dana confronted me. She was standing in the cone of light cast by the bridge lamp and she took my breath away.

I had suspected from her manner that something extra special was brewing, but I wasn't prepared for this. If she had planned to knock me silly, she had succeeded. I knew that this was being staged for my benefit, and that what she wanted was a verdict, so I tore my eyes away from her face and tried, in my masculine ignorance, to concentrate on her costume.

She was wearing a purple dress. Undoubtedly the modiste who designed it wouldn't have called it purple. She'd have used whatever the trick name was they were using for purple. The portion of it that was in shadow looked midnight black, but wherever the light touched it, it looked like moonlight on water.

The top part was one of those strapless arrangements which defy the law of gravity. It emphasized the smooth whiteness of her throat and shoulders and the curve of her breasts. Deep folds, crossed in front and pulled snugly into the waist, didn't do any injustice to the charms they only partially concealed.

Below the waistline, the skirt billowed out: smooth purple satin, and stiff, crisp net in alternating sections. It spread wider and wider as it approached the floor. I knew that it was designed to swirl away from her body while she was dancing. At the moment, it fell soft and full about her feet.

Long purple gloves covered her hands and arms, up to the

115

line of the bodice. But the ultimate artistry was achieved by two touches—dramatic in their simplicity.

Peeping from under the hem of her skirt were dancing pumps of ruby-red satin, and fastened in the mass of tight little curls at the side of her head was an enameled clip which shaded from deepest purple to the same vivid red.

She smiled and turned. She turned slowly, like a model. She finished the manœuver and her eyes rested on mine. I said, "Good Lord! you're beautiful!"

Her eyes sparkled. She said, "Go on."

"There's nothing to go on with. Except that you've been holding out on me. I never dreamed you could look like that."

"Like what?"

"Like . . . like . . . how can I say it? Like something out of this world. Like an angel who has been living on a diet of nectar. And at the same time like a warm, exciting woman."

"The gown, Kirk. What about the gown?"

"I—I don't know. It isn't the gown and it isn't you. It's the combination. It's the ultimate carried to infinity."

She threw herself into my arms and did things that I liked. She said anxiously, "You really mean that, darling?"

"Of course I mean it. What's it all about?"

She stood up again and backed into the light. "I've been worried. All my life I've been sold on the idea that purple simply wasn't for me. My dress designer insisted on making this for me with the understanding that if it weren't becoming—the color, I mean—I wouldn't owe her a cent. That's why I asked you to come over. The dress was delivered less than two hours ago. I want to wear it at the dinner show tonight . . . but only if I'm sure it looks right."

I tried to tell her how right I thought it looked. She said, "I was concerned about the color. When you've always believed you couldn't wear something, and then you consider stepping out on a dance floor in that color . . . well, you're afraid you might look grotesque."

I was amused. She had counted so much on my verdict. I talked for a long time. I talked until I was fresh out of words. It took me that long to convince her that the color was right for her, and that she'd create a sensation.

She finally got the idea. She was walking on air when she

went back into the bedroom to change into street clothes. When she returned, she had a long, wide pasteboard box under her arm. The new purple dress, the shoes and the hair ornament were in it. We taxied to the club.

There weren't many people inside. We walked toward the rear, and somebody called me. It was John Ferguson. He was dining with another man at a wall table. They stood up and Ferguson introduced the other man to Dana. She chatted briefly, then excused herself and started for her dressing room.

Ferguson invited me to join them for dinner. I said No, and explained about the skating party. Just to make it good, Agnes Sheridan chose that moment to come in, carrying her skates which were attached to white skating shoes.

Maybe I was in an unusually appreciative mood tonight, but Agnes looked prettier than I'd thought was possible. She had on some sort of a brown tweed suit with a white sweater underneath. Her beaver coat was swung over her shoulders with the sleeves dangling empty at her sides. A tiny little white hat—a beanie—was perched jauntily on her head and, instead of gloves, she was wearing white, woolly mittens.

There were more introductions. Then Agnes and I got away and made for my corner table near the corridor. Ferguson smiled and made a flattering comment about the work I was doing for him. I liked that. I liked Ferguson. I liked his friend. I liked almost everybody.

Dana showed up in the archway and grabbed Agnes. She said, "Better bring your skates back to my dressing room. We'll pick them up after the show. And besides . . ."

"Besides," I said, "she wants your opinion about a gown."

The two girls disappeared. The show had started by the time Agnes came back. She had seen the purple dress and was slightly hysterical about it.

Just to make it one big, happy family, Candy Livingston swept in at the head of a party of six. Once again she grabbed the attention which rightly belonged to the show girls. She saw us and came over. She insisted that we join her. I went into my routine. No could do. Skating party. I didn't ask her to go with us. There was too much danger that she'd accept.

As the time for the Ricardo & Dana act approached, I found myself getting excited. Suppose I'd been wrong? Suppose Agnes and the modiste had been wrong? I was commencing to understand how such a thing could be important.

The emcee gave them the usual ritzy build-up. I deliberately had refrained from looking at Dana while she was waiting for her cue. My first glimpse of her was on the floor, in Ricardo's arms, the big spot beating down on the purple gown.

There was a hush over the place, then a spontaneous burst of applause. It wasn't the dancing; they hadn't gone far enough into the number. It must be the gown. I felt relieved.

They went through three routines and finished to an ovation. While they were waiting to let the applause die down, Candy Livingston swept past our table and into the corridor. Headed for the powder room, I gathered, but I was resentful of the fact that she was walking out before the end of the act.

There was more applause after the encore number. The team took a half dozen bows, then I saw Ricardo go toward his dressing room. Dana stopped at our table. We all talked about the gown, and then Dana beckoned to Agnes. "Come on back while I change. You, Kirk, can join us in ten minutes."

The show was over. The regular orchestra was starting a loud, thumping rhumba which the relief combo would finish.

The girls went into the dim, drafty corridor and turned left. Then something happened. Something loud, but not too loud. There was no mistaking that sound.

It was a shot.

There was a split-second of silence, then a choked scream. I was on my feet. I knew who had screamed. It was Dana.

People were pouring into the corridor when I got there. Waiters from the kitchen; men and women from the rest rooms. We all moved toward the same place.

The first person I saw was Dana. She was standing motionless, her eyes wide with terror.

Agnes Sheridan was on the floor.

She was wearing a white sweater under her tweed costume. But the sweater wasn't all white. There was a reddish-brown

118

spot under the left breast. One leg was bent under her. The left arm was stretched out, the fingers curled.

I didn't have to look twice to know that she was dead.

There was a lot of talking and pushing. Somebody said, "Call the police" and somebody else said, "Get a doctor!"

I heard a voice at my elbow. It was Candy Livingston's voice. It said, "Oh my God! . . ."

My eyes went to the end of the corridor. The door of Ricardo's dressing room was closed. Dana's door was slightly ajar. And while I was watching it, it opened.

Ricardo came out. Not out of his own dressing room. He came out of Dana's room.

He stared at the crowd. He moved swiftly and joined the people who hovered over Agnes Sheridan's body.

Ricardo's eyes met mine. I saw something there. Something I didn't like. I got a sickish feeling in the pit of my stomach. I thought, "Ricardo shot Agnes. But he didn't mean to. The person he intended to kill was Dana."

XX

THE CORRIDOR back of the Club Caliente had seen a lot of things in its day, but it was seeing something new now.

Jamming into it were all sorts of people: waiters, bus boys, chorus girls, guests who were calm and guests who were hysterical. There was the odor of kitchen, the blending of assorted and expensive perfumes. And over everything that oppressive pall which is invariably associated with death.

I edged over to Dana. I took her hand. It was icy. Apparently she hadn't moved since Agnes Sheridan had been killed. Her body was like a statue: a cold, beautiful statue. I said softly, "Get a grip on yourself, sweetheart. The cops will be here in a minute and they're going to ask you a lot of questions."

My timing was good. Two uniformed men barged in. One of them said, "Somebody must've phoned Homicide already. We'll wait."

For the moment, until the arrival of the first detective, this man was in charge. He liked it. He stared sternly at the circle of pinched, strained faces and asked, "Anybody touched this body?"

Heads were shaken, but nobody spoke.

"Any idea who done the shooting?"

Nobody had any idea who done it. I pressed my body against Dana's. She was beginning to relax. Not much, but a little.

There was another commotion. Two men in plain clothes came in. One of them was big and beefy and young. He had expressionless eyes—like agates. The other was stubby and broad and had the blackest hair I had ever seen. It was Detective Lieutenant Max Gold. He told the patrol-car boys that he'd take over. Then he looked down at what had been Agnes Sheridan and at the ring of faces which peered at him with that tense eagerness which indicated that they expected him to produce a rabbit.

He told them who he was. He asked whether anyone could tell him what had happened, but nobody could—whereupon he looked a trifle uncertain. I fancied I would, too, even if I were Mister Scotland Yard. I wouldn't know where to begin.

Then Gold saw me. He said, "Always on the spot, ain't you, Douglas?" For some reason it struck me as remarkable that he should remember my name.

He shot a lot of verbal arrows into the air. The sum total of results was slightly less than nothing. It was apparent that nobody except Dana had been in the corridor when Agnes was shot. Dana was the only one except myself and Candy Livingston who recognized the dead girl. So we were elected. I took note of the fact that Ricardo hadn't spoken. He hadn't admitted that he knew Agnes Sheridan.

Gold said, "Where's a good place to talk?" He was looking at Dana when he said it.

"My dressing room?" Dana's rising inflection made it more of a question than a suggestion.

Gold told the two patrolmen and the other detective to start taking down names and addresses. He announced that nobody was to leave the Caliente until he gave the word.

Some more people joined the crowd in the corridor. There was a medical examiner, a photographer, a fingerprint man, and a fellow who started taking measurements. Their scrutiny of Agnes's body was startlingly impersonal. They herded the guests and waiters and bus boys and chorus girls back into the club. Ricardo went with them. So did Candy Livingston.

Gold said, "Let's go, Miss Warren."

I asked, "May I come along?"

"Why not?" There was a suggestion of amusement in his eyes. "For a nice solid citizen, Douglas, you sure get around."

We went into Dana's dressing room and closed the door. The first thing Gold spied was Agnes's skates. He asked about them, and Dana told him about the skating party we had planned. Gold said, "So that's why she was dressed like that, huh?"

Dana sat stiffly on the little chair in front of her make-up table. I perched gingerly on the edge of a ridiculous white satin easy chair. Gold stood in the corner where he could watch us and look around the dressing room at the same time.

I looked around, too. I was remembering that Ricardo had come out of this room a few seconds after Agnes had been killed. The fact that he had come here, instead of going to his own dressing room, might mean anything or nothing.

Gold was friendly, but not too much so. I asked whether we might have a drink all 'round, and he shook his head. I figured he was interested in our emotions, and didn't want to induce any artificial relaxation.

Dana started to shiver. She had on practically nothing from the midriff up, so I took her coat off its hanger and draped it around her shoulders. She thanked me, and patted my hand.

Gold started questioning her. He wasn't acting tough. He was just an efficient man doing an efficient job.

"You say you and Miss Sheridan started for this dressing room right after you finished your act, Miss Warren. She had left her skates here. You stepped into the corridor together. What happened?"

Dana said, "We started toward my room. We got about halfway down the corridor when I heard the gun go off."

"How did you know it was a gun?"

"I didn't. I just heard a noise."

"Did you see anything?"

121

"No."

"You got any idea which way the bullet came from?"

"No."

He shrugged. "We can find that out easy enough. The point is that since you and her was walking in this direction, you must have been facing this way. Right?"

Dana nodded.

"When you started out," Gold continued, "was Miss Sheridan acting unusual? Like she was afraid of something?"

"No. Nothing like that."

"What was she talking about?"

"My gown." Dana touched the gleaming satin of her skirt. "She was saying how much she liked it."

Max looked her over. "It's swell," he said. "I can't hardly blame her. So there come a noise, which you didn't know was a shot. What happened then, Miss Warren?"

"Agnes stopped talking. I had walked ahead about two steps. I turned and looked at her."

"You still didn't see nobody?"

"Not then. Later, the corridor got crowded."

"Did Miss Sheridan make any exclamation?"

"No. She just stood there and then she commenced to sag. All of a sudden she pitched forward, and after she fell she rolled over on her back. The blood was beginning to show . . ."

Dana stopped. She wasn't too far from a crack-up. Gold said, "Take it easy. No sense punishing yourself."

Dana thanked him with a nod. "I'm all right, lieutenant."

"Sure, I know. But it's tough being in on something like this." He asked some more questions: How long had Dana and Agnes known each other; where and how had they met; what did Dana know about Agnes's private life. He didn't seem enthusiastic. He said, "I always draw blanks."

I leaned forward. "Look, may I ask Miss Warren a couple of questions? You can stop her from answering any of them if you wish. After I'm through, I'll explain what I'm driving at."

He gave that a going over. "I don't see no harm in it."

I made my voice as gentle as possible. "Think carefully, Dana. Up to the moment you heard the shot, how close had you and Agnes been to each other?"

She looked at me in surprise. "Close? Why, as close as people would naturally walk, I suppose."

"That means very close? Almost shoulder to shoulder?"

"I guess so. I don't remember exactly."

"But if you hadn't been normally close, you'd be likely to remember that, wouldn't you?"

"Y-y-yes, I suppose to. I noticed as soon as she dropped behind me. But that wasn't until after I heard the shot."

"About the shot: You didn't see any flash?"

"No, I told the lieutenant . . ."

"Be patient. Did the shot seem to come from real close or from a distance? By a distance, I mean maybe twenty feet."

She concentrated. Then she shook her head. "I don't know, Kirk. When I heard the noise, it seemed to come from everywhere at once. As though there were a dozen echoes."

"Did you notice that your dressing room door was slightly open?"

"No."

I spread my hands in a helpless gesture. I said, "If you want me to explain, lieutenant . . ."

He said, "In a minute. Meanwhile, I'd like to ask you a couple of questions, Douglas." His manner was calculating. "In the crowd back yonder, didn't I see Candy Livingston?"

"Yes," I said. "She was there."

"You know her?"

"Yes."

"How well?"

Dana and I glanced at each other. I said carefully, "That's an odd question, lieutenant."

"Not so odd. As a matter of fact, I'll lay a few cards on the table. It wasn't too long ago that a babe was knocked off in your apartment. I told you then, and I repeat, I wasn't sold on the idea you done it, but I thought you knew more than you were telling. I still think so. Anyway, we sort of kept check on you. One of the things we know is that you and Candy Livingston have been friendly."

I said, "I'm friendly with a lot of people."

"Candy ain't a lot of people. She's somebody extra special. Where she happens to be, things usually happen. Do you know where Livingston was when Miss Sheridan was killed?"

"No. Not exactly."

"What does that mean?"

"Well, just before Ricardo & Dana left the floor, Miss Livingston went into the powder room."

"Did you see her go in?"

"No. She went into the corridor, and I presumed . . ."

"Yeh. But you ain't positive. The important point is that she went into the corridor while Ricardo & Dana was still dancing." He looked down at the toes of his highly polished shoes. "Did Candy know about this here skating party?"

"Yes."

"Did you maybe see her come *out* of the ladies' room?"

"No. I just saw her in the crowd after it happened."

"Mmmmm!" Gold's smile was rather bleak. "Wasn't Candy Livingston kinda cut in the head about you? Wasn't she making a play?"

I hesitated. The question was embarrassing, but there was something more important than embarrassment to cope with now.

I said, "She seemed to like me."

"How much?"

I said, "You're shoving me, lieutenant. I can't give you an honest answer because I'm not sure. I always thought that I interested her because I was something different. I was the nice solid young man with some sort of a professional future, and she had just had a rather unpleasant experience . . . that kidnaping business."

Gold made a sound popularly associated with the Bronx. "That story she tells about being kidnaped—it stinks."

XXI

Max gold's remark brought me up short. I said, "You mean Candy wasn't kidnaped?"

"I mean we don't think so. She goes away without leaving word, which ain't unusual. She makes all the ransom arrangements over the telephone. The day after the money is paid— a half million smackers—she comes back, bright and chipper.

She tells a story that's as full of holes as Swiss cheese. What she describes is an abduction that turns into kidnaping. She says she was treated wonderful. She describes a guy to us that could be anybody you pass on the street. She gives us a name that means even less than that. The only way she slips is that she mentions New Jersey. That makes it interstate and brings in the F.B.I. boys.

"They question her, too. She hands them the same double-talk. When they try to pin her down, she clams up. She makes it clear that she doesn't want this guy found and prosecuted. So even if he was found, she'd be a hostile witness. No indictment we could bring could be made to stick. So the case is shoved into a file to be pulled out when, as, and if needed. She makes us play it her way, but we don't have to believe her. It's a helluva life, bein' a cop."

I made some inane remark which didn't mean anything. Then Gold asked abruptly, "You ever get a hunch on who put that hundred thousand in your account?"

I shook my head.

"Maybe it was Candy Livingston," he suggested. "That'd be just so much bird gravel to her."

I said, "I didn't know her then."

"So what?" So maybe she knew you. Maybe you looked like somebody she'd like to give a hundred thousand dollars to."

"That's silly, lieutenant."

"Okay," he said placidly. "I just happened to be thinking that the dates were all bunched up along there. Also that when a dame like Livingston makes a play for a guy, he usually has more than you've got."

I said, "Aren't we getting pretty far away from what just happened out yonder?"

"That's what I'd like to know."

Dana said, "You don't think Candy . . . ?"

"Ma'am, I don't think nothing! Candy was here tonight. If she had any reason, she could have done the shooting; just like, if she had of had a reason, she could of slipped Douglas that hundred thousand." He put up his hand. "Don't say it, Miss Warren. I'm six jumps ahead of you. Candy didn't have no reason. Okay. But who did? I'm just tossing

125

her around in my peanut brain until something better comes along."

I said quietly, "Maybe I can give you something better."

"Yeah . . . ?" His voice didn't change, and his eyes were still calm and friendly. But I knew he was listening hard.

I didn't look at Dana. I wanted her to hear what I had to say, and knew it would be tough. But I had to say it anyway.

I said, "I may as well start off by reminding you that I'm in love with Miss Warren, and want to marry her. Therefore you can discount what I'm going to say as coming from a prejudiced witness. What I'm driving at is that I think the time has come to quit holding out on you, which I only did because I couldn't find anything solid on which to base my suspicions."

"Holding out ain't so good," commented Max.

I started to tell him about Ricardo. As soon as I mentioned the name, Dana drew in her breath sharply and said, "Kirk! Don't!" and I said, "I've got to, honey. You'll see why."

I told Max Gold everything I knew about Ricardo. I told him about falling in love with Dana and the way Ricardo had reacted. I told him about the missing luck piece and how it had turned up in my apartment. I gave him the battered coin. I told him that, to my knowledge, Ricardo had never been in my apartment. I told him about our fight at the rehearsal hall. I told him that only recently Dana had notified Ricardo that she was quitting the act, regardless. The one opinion I expressed was that nothing could hit Ricardo much harder than that, because his profession—and the position he held in it—probably meant more to him than anything else in the world, and that Dana would be almost impossible to replace.

Gold let me finish. He gave it plenty of time to sink in. He said, "Why are you telling me this now?"

"Because . . ." I hesitated, and he encouraged me with, "Keep going, Douglas."

"All right," I said. "Here's the last touch. When Ricardo & Dana left the floor tonight, Miss Warren stopped at our table. Ricardo went into the corridor. His dressing room is right across the hall from this one. When I heard the shot, I ran into the corridor. I saw that door open and Ricardo came out."

126

"Out of Miss Warren's dressing room?"

"Yes. Out of this room we're in now."

"Did he have a gun?"

"I didn't see any."

"Did he know Miss Sheridan?"

"Casually."

"Why would he shoot her?"

"I don't think he would. Except by accident."

Gold ground the fire from the end of his cigarette. He nodded thoughtfully. "That adds up better than some of the ideas I've had, Douglas. You figure Ricardo was sore about a lot of things, but mostly because he was going to lose an ace dance partner. He was waiting in her dressing room. He saw her coming with somebody else and took a shot at her. Only he ain't so expert, so he blasts Agnes Sheridan instead of his wife. Is that what you think?"

Dana was trying to say something. She was trembling again. I said, "I don't think anything, lieutenant."

"Then why are you telling me?"

"Because," I said carefully, "I believe that whoever did the killing was shooting at Dana—not at Miss Sheridan, And I'm afraid—for her."

Dana stood up. "I can't think it was Ricardo. He's tough, but I don't believe . . . Does it strike you as reasonable, lieutenant?"

Gold said, "Yes. And No. There's enough motive, but the way it was done—there's lots of flaws in it. Even if he wanted to kill you, it doesn't seem hardly probable he'd have gone through with it when he saw you wasn't alone. Of course, there's still another angle. An amateur gets himself nerved up to do something. He knows he'll never get that hopped up again. So he lets fly anyway." Gold walked to the door and called somebody. There was a brief, whispered conference, then he came back to us. "They'll case Ricardo's room. I'll give him a going over later." He turned his attention to me. "Ricardo was making a play for Candy Livingston, wasn't he?"

I said, "I don't know."

"I got reason to think he was. If she liked you, that would be something else that wouldn't make Ricardo happy." He shook his head. "Jeez! feller, you sure got yourself in the middle of a mess, didn't you?"

"Yes. But that isn't what worries me. I'm concerned about Dana. If what happened tonight was an attempt on her life, it might happen again. There must be some sort of way to guard against that."

Dana said, "I can't believe Ricardo could hate me that much, or that I'd be so valuable to him as a dance partner. I can give you an alphabetical list of all his faults. But I can't see him as the killer type."

Max said dryly, "You'd be surprised, Ma'am, what kind of folks can get a sudden itch to commit homicide." He turned his attention to the luck piece again. "So he was sore when he found it was missing, huh?"

Dana said, "Yes," and I said, "Miss Warren told me he seemed more upset than the loss of a luck piece could possibly explain."

"And Ricardo commenced getting real ugly as of then?"

Dana nodded. Gold said, "Some guys is superstitious as hell." He looked across at me. "This thing was found under the edge of the rug in your apartment, Douglas?"

"Yes. Under the couch."

"You should of told me." Gold's voice was gently reproving. "It's tough enough to go places even when we know everything. Having somebody hold out . . . well, that ain't so good."

"I'm sorry. But you understand why I did it."

"I know. The scandal."

"I was trying to find out if Ricardo had ever known Ethel Brower. If it turned out that he had, I'd have come to you with the whole story."

"I'm a funny guy," Max said. "I like to do my own thinking. How much do you know about this Agnes Sheridan?"

"Very little. Except that she worked as a nurse's aide at the McKinley Hospital."

"I liked her," volunteered Dana. "She seemed like a thoroughly nice person."

"She ever tell you anything about herself?"

"No. I gathered that she lived alone, that she had a comfortable income, and that she was a very patriotic person."

128

Gold shrugged. "We oughn't to have much trouble check-ing on her." He walked to the door. He paused with his hand on the knob and said, "Thanks to both of you."

"What do we do now?"

"How should I know. Whatever you like."

"We can go?"

"Why not?" His lips spread in a broad grin. "But get this, Douglas: Next time you get hold of any information, give me a thought. You ain't got any idea how much it helps."

He stepped into the corridor, closing the door behind him. I stood up and put my arms around Dana. She said, "You don't really think Ricardo did it, do you?"

"I don't know what to think. I only know I'm afraid. I know I hate to have you go through things like this . . ."

She leaned back in my arms and stared hard at me. She said, in a tight little voice, "You're afraid for me, aren't you, Kirk?"

"Naturally."

"And I'm afraid for you." I looked puzzled, and she went on: "It all seems to center around you: the money in the bank, the dead girl in your apartment, someone trying to kill Arthur Maybank for no apparent reason except that he is your friend, the thing tonight—whether it was meant for Agnes or for me. It's you I'm afraid for, Kirk . . . can't you see that?"

I shook my head. I told her she was crazy, but I knew she wasn't. I tried to quiet her. I held her close. I told her how much I loved her.

I finally succeeded in easing the tension. She started to cry. She cried like a little girl. Softly. And I stood there patting her and feeling rotten.

I got her quieted down. I sat uncomfortably while she went behind the screen and changed.

We left the dressing room together. Someone told us that the supper show had been called off.

The corridor looked normal. Even Agnes Sheridan had gone. They had taken her body to the morgue.

XXII

I TOOK DANA home, and said I was going downstairs for some cigarettes. I went to the nearest drugstore and bought a mild sedative—the sort you can get without a prescription. When I got back with it, Dana had undressed. All I could see was a housecoat and a pair of cute little mules.

I gave her the sedative. I offered to sleep on the couch, but she wasn't having any. She insisted she'd be all right. I made her promise to telephone me in case she wasn't.

I stuck around until she started to get drowsy. Then I kissed her good night and walked out, closing the door gently. I started across town on what I knew would be an unpleasant mission.

The accident room of the McKinley looked only a shade more unclean than it had on my first visit. The same girl found Arthur talking with a big, burly man who turned out to be the ambulance driver. He looked like the sort of lad who loved his job. Going through traffic and under red lights at fifty seemed to be just about what he had been designed for.

Arthur was on duty. He smiled when he saw me and walked forward with his hand out.

I told him about Agnes as gently as I could. I spared him the details. I said I believed that whoever had done it was really shooting at Dana. That left Agnes just as dead.

He took it pretty hard. His weak mouth trembled. I felt like a heel, as though I were personally responsible. He asked me a lot of questions, and about all I could do was to tell him I didn't know the answers. I stayed until an accident call came in. Arthur went out with the ambulance driver. I told him to keep a grip on himself. Then I went home.

I didn't have much luck getting to sleep. When I finally dozed off, I didn't enjoy it because my dreams were unpleasant. I woke at nine, drank some coffee, lighted a cigarette and retrieved my two morning papers from outside the door.

The killing of Agnes Sheridan made gusty reading, in spite

130

of the fact that the reporters hadn't had much to go on. They pulled out all the stops in describing the "exclusive" Club Caliente. I never had been able to figure what made a place like that exclusive unless it was the prices, but that's the way it was invariably described.

Nobody knew anything about Agnes; they hadn't had time to check on her. One account described her as a "vivid, vital, beautiful brunette," which was pretty good going, considering.

The mystery angle was neat. No motive. No suspect. No gun. I could see that Lieutenant Max Gold of the homicide squad had told the reporters precisely what they'd find out anyway, and not another word.

Neither Dana nor Ricardo were mentioned, except as the stars of the de luxe show. Candy's name wasn't there. Neither was mine. It was a nice story. But when you had finished reading it you hadn't read anything.

Shortly before nine-thirty, I telephoned the office and told them I wouldn't be in. I kidded a little with the switchboard operator, but I don't think I was as funny as Jack Benny.

I knew what I was going to do. It didn't matter what it was, except that I felt the time had come for me to do something.

The more I thought, the more convinced I became that the bullet which had killed Agnes had been intended for Dana. I thought back over all the things that had happened, all the things that had been said, and one item stuck.

Max Gold had his eye on Candy Livingston. Max was a shrewd detective. He had been interested in Candy's presence at the club the previous night. He had said that her kidnaping story was a phony. He suggested that she might have been connected with the hundred thousand dollars which somebody had stuck into my puny account at the bank.

That checked with a lot of other things. I didn't know where Candy fitted in, but I felt certain she knew a lot she wasn't telling. Maybe I was the guy who could induce her to talk. I'd be rough or affectionate or whatever the situation called for. I had a definite job. That job was to protect Dana from whatever might be threatening her.

Fired with enthusiasm and high purpose, I telephoned Candy's apartment. A cute little feminine voice answered and identified itself as belonging to Miss Livingston's personal

131

maid. I asked for Candy, and the maid said that she wasn't there. She said that Miss Livingston had left more than a half hour before. No, she wasn't sure where Miss Livingston had gone. Candy had said she'd be back late that night or early the next morning. I left my name and number.

I phoned Dana. She was out, too. I went to her apartment house and waited in the lobby. She came in about two o'clock in the afternoon. She looked pale and drawn. We went up to her apartment and started to fix up a little lunch.

She said, "I saw Ricardo this morning. He telephoned me."

"And . . . ?"

"Kirk! I'm sure he had nothing to do with that shooting. And he's terrified. The police questioned him for hours. He says it doesn't matter how innocent he is, they've built up a strong circumstantial case against him. I've never before seen him frightened. It isn't a pretty sight."

I tried hard to be sorry for Ricardo, but wasn't very successful. I was nervous about Dana meeting him. Of course, I believed that Ricardo was messed up in this thing, but Dana thought otherwise. So, naturally, she wouldn't be afraid of him. There didn't seem to be much I could do about it.

I left her when it came time to go to the club. I went to my place and did a lot of reading without absorbing anything. I was in bed by ten o'clock and asleep shortly after that. At three o'clock my telephone rang. I snapped on the reading lamp and said, "Hello."

It was Candy Livingston, bright and chipper as you please. She said, "I just got home and found your message. What gives?"

I made a date to see her at one o'clock the next afternoon. She didn't mention Agnes's death. I couldn't get anything over the telephone except that she was glad I had called her. I cut off and went back to sleep. I slept until ten o'clock.

The Wednesday morning papers had a brief mention of the Agnes Sheridan murder. No more than three sticks in length. Still no gun. Still no suspect. Everything just the same.

I went to the barber shop and demanded the works. When I left there I was slicked down beautifully and smelled like a tuberose. I reached Candy's apartment building five minute

132

late. Kirk Douglas, always socially correct. I was kidding myself along, but deep down inside I was nervous.

Candy answered my ring. I had anticipated a seductive negligee, but I didn't get it. What I did get was a nifty little house dress which was quite revealing despite its studied simplicity. She didn't look like the Candy Livingston of Cafe Society, but she was still blonde enough and gorgeous enough to knock your eye out.

She took my coat and hat and led me into the living room. The carpeting was so thick it tickled my ankles. At the end of the room two glass doors were open. The table had been set. Cocktails were already mixed. Candy said, "You'll probably be surprised as hell when I tell you we're alone. I let the servants go."

"Tomorrow is Thursday," I said. "They'd be off then anyway."

The lunch was simple and lovely. So were we. Candy was lovely and I was simple. We moved into the living room for coffee. She shoved a humidor at me, remembered how much sugar I liked in my coffee, and seated herself beside me on the couch.

I fancied that I detected amusement in her eyes. She said, "To what do I owe the honor of this visit, Mr. Douglas?"

I tried to match her mood. I said, "Perhaps I couldn't resist you any longer."

"I'm not buying that. The brilliant young architect doesn't prowl at midday without a reason."

"Haven't you ever been told that you're reason enough?"

"Not by you, I haven't." She leaned toward me, her expression serious. "It's about Monday night, isn't it?"

"Yes." I liked her directness. "That—and other things."

She said, "Take your time. We've got until tomorrow morning."

I said, "How well did you get to know Agnes Sheridan?"

"Not at all well. But I'm that sort of a person. Sudden intimacies. She seemed to like me, and I liked her. She was fun in her own intense sort of way. I enjoyed having her around."

"Did you ever visit her?"

"Never."

133

"She told you nothing about herself?"

"No. It wouldn't have been easy, anyway. I'm no good at butting into other people's affairs."

I said casually, "You were in the powder room when she was shot, weren't you?"

"Yes." She looked at me peculiarly. "Why do you ask that?"

"I saw you pass our table. I presumed—"

"But you weren't sure. You're trying to ask whether I was in the corridor. Well, I wasn't. I didn't kill her."

I said, "Wow! but you hit straight."

"Why not? You came here to question me; just why, I don't know. But since that's on your mind, you may as well play it across the board."

"You're a nice person, Candy," I said. "And you're making a tough job simple. First: Have you any theory about who killed Agnes, or why?"

"No."

"Okay. How do you feel about Dana?"

"I like her personally. And I'm jealous as hell."

I said, "I know you were kidding that night at my place . . ."

"I wasn't kidding. I'm in love with you."

I felt silly. And embarrassed. I said, "I think Agnes was killed by accident."

"I don't get it."

"I believe that whoever shot her meant to kill Dana."

Candy's eyes got big. "I still didn't do it. I'm not that type."

I was getting no less bewildered by the minute. The girl's directness intrigued me. I decided I'd better take full advantage of my opportunity. I said, "I've been talking to Max Gold about you. He's a lieutenant attached to the homicide squad of the New York police department."

"So what?"

"He doesn't hold you in very high esteem."

"Is that supposed to make me miserable?"

"Gold claims that your story about being kidnaped was a fake. The way he expressed it was, 'Her story stinks'."

She smiled. "He sounds like a wise guy."

134

"I believe he is. Really wise. Not just somebody who cracks that way."

"In other words: You believe him."

"I didn't say that. I don't know anything about it. I'm only asking."

"Why?"

"Because I'm worried. A lot of things have been happening all around me that don't make sense. I think you can supply some of the answers." I looked straight at her. "Were you really kidnaped."

"No."

"But you were away . . ."

"It was one of those things. I told you frankly that I was wild. Too much money; too little supervision. I met a man and fell for him. There wasn't anything new about that." She broke off suddenly. "I'm a damn fool to be telling this to *you*."

"Go ahead, please."

"I went away with this man. It was fun at first. Until I discovered that he was a prime louse. He was also a blackmailer. I'm moderately notorious, but that was one escapade I didn't care to see plastered all over the gossip pages. We cooked up the kidnaping story. It was designed as a face-saver for me. It was worth what it cost to get away from him."

I said, "Would you be willing to tell me his name?"

She hesitated, then said, "You know the man already. He's one of the cleverest confidence men in America. His name is John Ferguson."

XXIII

I SAT THERE gawking. I had come for information, and Candy had handed me a portion that I couldn't even begin to digest.

Ferguson! I hadn't figured him in this. He hadn't meant a thing to me other than a suave, distinguished-looking man who wanted to construct a beautiful office building. He had selected a brilliant young architect to design something that would set a new style in office buildings. He built me up in

135

my own estimation, and now he was letting me down by turning out to be a common crook. I had a brief, consoling remembrance of what the Big Boss had said: that my sketches and ideas were excellent; that even if Ferguson didn't approve them, some other client would.

Candy's sapphire eyes never left my face. She was enjoying the situation. She said. "Is it all clear to you now, Kirk?"

"It would be—if I could understand it."

"Which part of it?"

I reached for a cigarette with fingers which were far from steady. She started talking again. "I usually take what I want," she said quietly. "There was a time not so long ago when I wanted John Ferguson. His appearance fooled me. Underneath he's just a cheap, tawdry heel."

I was trying to fit the pieces together. I said, "I introduced you to him. You accepted the introduction."

"What would you expect me to do? Say, 'Oh, I've met Mr. Ferguson. I played house with him for quite a while, and then paid a half million dollars to get rid of him.' "

"I see your point."

"I'm not ashamed of many things, Kirk. But I am ashamed of the Ferguson episode." She toyed with an ebony-and-gold cigarette holder. "I'm quite a tramp, don't you think?"

"No!" I was vehement about it. "I think you're grand."

"And you like me better than ever before. But you've still got your passion under control."

I said, "I never was right bright."

My mind was playing with something else. I smiled at her and asked permission to go ahead with my quizzing. She shrugged and said, "Why not? What have I got to lose?"

I said, "Correct me if I'm wrong, but one idea has stuck with me. I've always had the rather absurd feeling that your meeting with me was not accidental."

She nodded. "Good going. It wasn't. I heard about you. I had you investigated. I learned that you were friendly with Ricardo & Dana. It was natural for me to go to the Caliente; half my life has been spent in joints like that. Meeting them was simple, too. But my real purpose was to meet you."

"Why?"

"Because a young lady named Ethel Brower had been

killed in your apartment. I read what the newspapers said about it. I wanted to estimate for myself whether you had killed her."

"You should have known better, Candy. If the police had thought so, they would have arrested me."

"That had me puzzled. But there was a possibility that I might discover things the police would miss. So I made my pitch."

I asked, "Why were you interested in Ethel Brower?"

"Because I had met her—when I was going through the kidnaping routine with John Ferguson."

"She was afraid of him?"

"I don't think so. But she visited his place in Jersey several times. I think she was the sweetheart of some man who worked for him."

"And when you discovered that she had been killed in my apartment . . . ?"

Candy laughed. She said, "Nobody can be as dumb as you act. Whatever was happening, Ethel Brower probably knew about it. After my release from what you might call durance vile, she turns up strangled in the apartment of a perfect stranger. The police believe your story that you don't know her. So if you hadn't killed her, it seemed to me that Ferguson was elected."

"Why?"

"Because the gentleman had always kept clear of the law. He has picked suckers like myself, people who were helpless because they were just a little bit over the line. As far as I know, he has no criminal record. He didn't propose to start one. It might have been that Ethel Brower tried to shake him down for some of the half million dollars I paid. Ferguson wouldn't like that. He could have followed her to your apartment, figuring that she was planning to sell out to you. He might have ended the argument in his own conclusive way. He has very strong hands."

I said, "Why me?"

She shook her head. "That's something I never could figure. Neither he nor Brower could have picked your name out of a hat. There's some connection that I don't savvy."

I got up and walked across the room. I leaned against the

mantel. I said, "Maybe I can help, Candy. On January 28th somebody deposited one hundred thousand dollars cash to my credit at the bank. I haven't the slightest idea who it was."

That seemed to floor her. She said slowly, "That was four days after my ransom money was paid. Three days after I returned without a wedding ring."

I fumbled around. "I always connected it with you."

"Why?"

"Because you're the first person I ever met who has that much money."

She laughed; a nice, clear laugh. She said, "It's the sort of thing I might have done. But I didn't. I hadn't even met you then."

"That's what I told Max Gold. But there's bound to be some tie-up."

"Probably. So I'll ask you again: Why you? And why do you stand over there when this couch is so comfortable?"

I grinned and seated mself beside her. I said, "Why are you being so frank with me? You must have a reason."

"I have." She didn't evade. "I'm frightened."

"Of what?"

"Ferguson. If he killed Ethel Brower it was for the purpose of keeping her mouth shut. He might do the same to me for the same reason."

I got her point. It seemed far-fetched, but so did a lot of other things that had been happening. While thoughts were chasing each other through my head, Candy started asking questions.

She said, "You think Agnes Sheridan was killed by accident, don't you?"

"Yes."

"You believe that whoever killed her meant to kill Dana Warren?"

"Yes."

"How long has Dana known Ferguson?"

"That's out. I introduced them to each other."

"You introduced me to Ferguson, too."

I said, "But look! That doesn't make sense. I didn't know
138

anything about you. I've known Dana for a long time. If she had ever met Ferguson before . . ."

"Okay. Don't get all het up about it. How about God's gift to the women . . . this Ricardo person? He might have been friendly with Ferguson without your knowing it, mightn't he?"

"It's possible."

"Ricardo knew where you lived. Ferguson could have found out that Ethel Brower was trying to contact you, and checked it up to Ricardo to argue her out of it."

"But why Ricardo?"

"Don't be simple," she said impatiently. "You and Dana are in love with each other. She's Ricardo's wife. In addition to that, she's a valuable piece of dancing property. It wouldn't be impossible that Ricardo is still in love with her. So suppose that Ferguson and Ricardo were friends. Suppose Ricardo suggested you as the fall guy? The hundred thousand dollars you had suddenly acquired would be difficult to explain. Ricardo would have a lot less to worry about if you were out of the picture. Maybe that isn't the best answer in the world, but it's the best we've thought of yet."

I could have dressed her story up. I could have told her that Ricardo had just learned that Dana was quitting the act—and him—no matter what happened. I could have told about his luck piece being found in my apartment. I could have suggested that, if Ricardo already had one murder on his hands, it wouldn't have been too difficult to nerve himself to commit a second.

I could have told her all that. But I didn't. Unless or until I found out that there had been contact between Ferguson and Ricardo previous to the Brower incident, it seemed hardly fair. It put me in the position of fitting facts to theories; of merely trying to prove a point.

We did a lot more talking. For all Candy's lightness, I saw that she was frightened. I said finally, "You've given me a lot of information. What do you want me to do with it?"

"Whatever you think best."

"That really puts me on the spot. I might make a bad guess.

139

"I'll take a chance." Her sense of humor came to the rescute. "I've been doing that pretty much all my life."

It was dusk when I got up to go. Candy helped me with my coat. She said, "Would it hurt much to kiss me?"

I put my arms around her. I kissed her. I did a pretty good job of it. It was she who broke away. She said, "Why didn't somebody tell me these things?"

I stepped into the hall and heard her close the door behind me. I rode down to the street level. I went to a drugstore, telephoned the homicide squad and asked for Lieutenant Max Gold. He was there. I said I wanted to see him, and he said he thought he'd be able to take it. I grabbed a taxi and gave the address: 230 West 20th Street.

The room in which Gold received me wasn't much. But it was businesslike. He said, "Let's have it."

I gave him the works—from the moment I stepped into Candy's apartment up to five minutes before I left. When I finished he looked at me a long time. Then he said, "That's a nice shade of lipstick you're wearing. But it looks better on a blonde."

I blushed and rubbed my lips and didn't say anything. He said, "Nice going, kid. I didn't think you had it in you." Then he drummed on the desk top with broad, strong fingers. "It adds up cute," he commented. "My bet is John Ferguson."

I remained silent.

"We know a lot about Ferguson," Max went on. "He's a smart cookie. Never picks a victim who isn't willing to take the best of it. We've never been able to cook up an indict·ment that would stick. Like this Candy Livingston thing: the victims are reluctant to testify. But the rest of it checks."

"Not all of it," I said. "Unless you're willing to concede that whoever killed Agnes Sheridan was really trying to get Dana."

He smiled thinly. "Even that checks," he said placidly "We just got our final reports on Agnes. They're interesting."

He took his time. I knew it would be big, but even so wasn't prepared for what he told me.

"This is what you might call the missing link," he said quietly. "Agnes Sheridan was John Ferguson's wife."

140

XXIV

Lieutenant max gold was having himself quite a time. He had let fly with both barrels, and now he leaned back in his creaky swivel chair to watch the effect on me.

I made a rather profane remark which indicated the measure of my astonishment. Then I laughed. Not much: just a little. He said, "What's funny?"

"I'm thinking about two introductions. I introduced Ferguson to Candy Livingston, who was his ex-gal friend. They were as formal and as blank as that wall in back of you. Ditto with Ferguson and Agnes. 'How do you do, Mr. Ferguson.' 'Delighted to meet you, Miss Sheridan.' And she was his wife."

Gold said, "They weren't working at it. They separated years ago. He's been sending her an adequate income."

I said, "Where does she fit in?"

"She's dead. That might mean something."

"You're miles ahead of me."

"Look . . ." His manner was that of a teacher explaining something to a small—and not too bright—pupil. "Candy Livingston ran off with John Ferguson. But before they eloped Ferguson must have known Candy, and it ain't unreasonable to suppose that Agnes knew that he knew her. As I remember your story, Agnes was in the Club Caliente when Candy accepted the introduction to Ferguson. Being a smart babe, we can sorta take it for granted that she smelled a mice. So what does she do? She cultivates Candy. And why? Because if there's been a half-million-dollar touch, she figures she might cut in on it. Follow me?"

"I'm with you this far."

"Naturally, Ferguson savvies what's going on. If my guess is correct, he doesn't like it. So he knocks Agnes off."

I thought that one over. I said, "I took it for granted that whoever shot Agnes was really after Dana Warren."

"You may be right, Douglas. I'm not going out on a limb. I'm just giving you a new thought to stew over."

141

I said, "Ferguson was in the club the night Agnes was killed. He knew we were going skating after the dinner show. Where was he at the moment the shooting occurred?"

"He's got a perfect alibi—too perfect. The man he was with says Ferguson never left the table until after the shooting. I never trust anything that neat."

"Then your bet is Ferguson?"

"My hunch is that way. Ricardo ties up nice, but not as nice as Ferguson. I wouldn't be too surprised if it turned out to be Ricardo, but my money rides the other way."

I asked, "How about the Ethel Brower killing?"

"What we figured for Ricardo could also apply to Ferguson. He and the Brower dame knew each other. He wouldn't have liked it if she spilled to you. Ricardo might have passed his information along to Ferguson instead of using it himself." He smiled a tight little smile. "That's the trouble with a murder like this, Douglas: sometimes you got more suspects than you want."

"But you still think it was Ferguson?"

"It looks that way—Yes."

"Why not arrest him?"

"For what?"

I made an impatient gesture. "Murder, for one thing."

Max Gold shook his head. "He could beat that rap, easy. The way things stand now, we haven't even got any good circumstantial evidence. There ain't any sense charging him with something until you figure you got a good chance to prove it."

"I don't see it that way. You could prove he kidnaped Candy Livingston. Once you did that, the rest would fit."

"Ferguson didn't kidnap Candy. He can prove it."

"How?"

"By you. The defense would get you on the stand and make you chirp. Being fairly honest, you'd have to repeat what Candy told you. So it wasn't a kidnaping."

I said, "Ferguson still got the half million dollars, didn't he?"

His bright eyes got brighter. "That money was just a gift from a girl friend. She gave it to him voluntarily."

I said, "Other things become clearer, now that I know

142

about Ferguson. Maybe he put the hundred thousand in the bank for me."

"What makes you think that?"

"I haven't any reason except that it ties in with the certainty that he took a lot of trouble to become friendly with me. He wasn't planning any office building, but he worked hard to make me think he was. I'm trying to figure why."

"You get the answer to that one, and I'll kiss you."

"That's something to look forward to." I grinned at him. "Ferguson's weakness is his interest in me. The answer must be hidden right there."

"Okay. You find it, and we'll slap him in the cooler so quick it'll make his hair curl." Max spread both of his powerful hands on the top of the desk. "It shapes up like Ferguson," he said. "I never was too willing to buy the Ricardo set-up. But even yet there's some angle that we've both missed. Maybe I can find it—maybe you can. But I want to warn you of one thing: Keep your guard up. Ferguson could be a cold, bad baby if he was pushed."

I left him and started walking. I got to Broadway and turned left. Far ahead the big signs were blazing against the frozen sky. I remembered that I hadn't eaten since lunch time. I dropped into a cafeteria which looked bright and warm. I made the rounds, grabbed myself a table near the window and tried to think by concentrating on the people who were hurrying by outside; a never-ending stream of people without personalities.

I was commencing to readjust my ideas. The more I thought, the less it looked like Ricardo. There were still a lot of things I couldn't understand, but the only real motives I'd ever been able to pin on Ricardo were jealousy—which I didn't believe—and bitterness over the fact that Dana was quitting the act.

The job of estimating Ferguson's position was simpler. Ethel Brower had seen him with Candy. It could be presumed that she knew that the kidnaping wasn't a kidnaping, and that the ransom money looked good to her. The same applied to Agnes. Ferguson wouldn't like women who knew too much. I put my money on Ferguson. What I wanted,

143

though, was to uncover the thing that was missing, so that the District Attorney could put him through the wringer.

I got a hunch. Arthur Maybank. He and Agnes had been playing around. How intimate they may have been, I didn't know. But they had been alone a lot and Agnes must have done some talking. Maybe she had dropped remarks which wouldn't mean a thing to Arthur, but might be significant in the light of what I knew now.

I thought of something else. Someone had tried to kill Arthur. That could come out Ferguson, too, without wasting a lot of logic. Ferguson might have thought that Agnes planned to upset his applecart. He might even have known that she had done too much talking already. It was better than any other theory I'd been able to concoct about the shooting of Arthur. It was worth discussing with him, at any rate.

I picked up my little pink check with the holes in it, and paid the cashier the amount opposite the last hole. I went to the nearest subway station and rode uptown. I walked across to the dreary edifice which was the McKinley Hospital.

Arthur was there. He was sitting in the accident room, doing nothing. He seemed glad to see me. I broke the news. He looked little, incredulous and frightened. He said, "And all the time I would have bet it was Ricardo."

"We all thought that," I agreed. "But we didn't know anything about Ferguson being a crook."

I felt sorry for Arthur. He looked scared to death. I told him what I wanted. I asked him to think back over everything he and Agnes had ever talked about. I explained that our answer might be hidden in some casual remark of hers which wouldn't have meant a thing until now.

We started checking. I hated to do it, because some of the things we discussed were intimate. There hadn't been many women in Arthur's life. I gathered that he was hit hard and that this, coming on top of her tragic death, was just a little more than he could take without danger of cracking.

In the middle of our conversation, an accident call came in. The burly ambulance driver appeared from nowhere and said, "Let's get goin', Doc."

Arthur looked at me helplessly. He said, "You'll wait here?"

"How long will you be?"

"I never know." He rushed across the room and button-holed a tall, slim, nice-looking boy who had just walked in. They talked earnestly for a few minutes, and then Arthur came back. "He's an interne," he explained. "He says he'll take over when I get back from this call. He's going upstairs now to change."

I said, "Suppose I go home, and you join me there. I'd like to telephone Dana. I haven't spoken to her all day."

He said he'd come to my apartment as soon as he was free. The ambulance sirened impatiently from the parking lot. Arthur scuttled off. I left the building and walked home.

I snapped on the reading lamp and settled myself in the easy chair under it. I picked up the telephone and called the Caliente. I had to wait a few minutes, but it was worth it. Dana's voice always sounded good. At the moment, it sounded better than that.

I told her I'd run into a lot of new and exciting information. She wanted to know all about it. I said I thought it would be better not to talk over the phone. Our connection was through the club switchboard, and I didn't know whether the operator might be listening in.

She saw my point, but it didn't make her any less curious. I told her I'd have lunch with her the next day and explain everything. She asked me to come over to the club and sit through the supper show, but I said that was impossible. I was waiting for Arthur, who would be along any minute. I had a lot of talking to do.

I told her that I loved her, and she said something along the same line. So I said it again, and she repeated on her end. We were very silly and adolescent. It still sounded good. I told her good night and hung up. I felt fine. I kept on feeling fine until the buzzer sounded.

I was surprised that Arthur could have completed his ambulance run so quickly. I went to the door and opened it. It wasn't Arthur.

It was John Ferguson.

He said, "May I come in?" and came in anyway. He took

145

off his overcoat and hat and dropped them on a chair. He was wearing a conservative oxford-gray suit, a white shirt and a plain blue necktie. He looked like a solid, prosperous citizen. He looked handsome and distinguished. He didn't look like a crook. Most particularly he didn't look like a murderer.

He dropped into a chair. I went back to where I had been sitting under the reading lamp. He smiled at me and I tried to smile back. He said I had a nice place, and I said I was glad he approved. I probably said a few other things, too, but I didn't know what they were because I was groping for the motive behind his visit.

I was afraid I knew. He had never before called on me. He wasn't the type to drop in unannounced. Something was on his mind, and I was fearful that it might be the same sort of something which had been on his mind at least twice before.

This looked as though it might be the pay-off. Ferguson was smart. He must have realized that by this time the police would have checked on Agnes and have discovered that she was his wife. How much else he knew, I couldn't be sure. The only thing I was sure of was that I was up against a man who might be desperate and certainly was dangerous. I recalled Max Gold's warning. It didn't make me feel any better.

Any hope I may have had was dispelled swiftly. He said, "You had quite a long visit with Candy Livingston today, didn't you, Kirk?"

I said, "How did you know that?"

"A little bird told me." His lips were smiling, but his eyes were hard and steady. "Was it pleasant?"

"Pleasant enough."

"An interesting person, Candy. Picturesques, glamorous, lovely. You must have had a very interesting conversation."

"More or less."

"What did you talk about?"

He didn't seem to be in a hurry. That suited me fine. I wasn't either. What I wanted was time. I knew something that he didn't. I knew that any minute now Arthur Maybank would be barging in. And while Arthur wasn't much of a physical specimen, I felt reasonably certain that Ferguson wouldn't take a potshot at me in the presence of any third person.

146

That he was there to do drastic things, I hadn't the slightest doubt. That he knew about my visit to Candy's apartment that afternoon only confirmed my belief. My job was to stall, to kill as much time as possible, and to pray that Arthur would show up before the zero hour.

I tried to act naturally. I tried to act like a man who didn't have anything on his mind except architecture. I tried to keep my eyes away from the second hand of the mantel clock as it crept around the dial.

I said, "We didn't talk about anything special."

"It wasn't important?"

"Of course not."

"Do you usually stay away from the office to make social calls on ravishing blondes?"

I gave a laugh that sounded like an echo of itself. I said, "You know how those things are."

"Do I?" Ferguson gave me a nice smile. "After you left Candy's apartment," he said genially, "did you enjoy your talk with that detective chap at the Homicide Bureau?"

I said, "He asked me to drop in. He wanted to ask me some questions."

"What kind of questions?"

"I don't think I ought to tell, do you?"

"Yes," he said. "I do."

Time was running out. I was sitting stiffly, my muscles tensed. The first move he made I'd act. I didn't believe I'd have much success, but at least I'd try.

Ferguson's face got hard. He said, "I'm asking you one more time, Kirk: What did you and Candy talk about? Specifically."

No more stalling. I could sense it. I decided to tell him a little bit of the truth. Just enough to keep him probing for more. I started to talk and then my heart jumped.

I hadn't heard the elevator stop. The first thing that happened was a key grating in the lock. The door opened. Arthur Maybank walked in. I didn't believe anybody could be as welcome.

Ferguson got up. So did I. It was good to be on my feet again. Arthur looked absurdly small with a big winter overcoat partly covering his hospital whites.

He looked at Ferguson. He looked at me. He looked at Ferguson again.

Then suddenly Arthur's face was contorted. His hand jumped out of his overcoat pocket. There was a gun in it. He aimed it at Ferguson and pulled the trigger. Ferguson bent over as though to pick up something. Then he pitched forward.

Arthur didn't move. He stood there with the gun in his hand, staring at the figure on the floor.

For an instant, I was paralyzed. Then I leaped across the room and snatched the gun from Arthur's cold, nerveless fingers. Someone banged on the door and I yelled, "Go away!" I suppose they went, because there was no more banging.

I went to the telephone and dialed Watkins 9-8242, which was the number of the homicide squad. I was lucky. Max Gold was there. I told him to come right up. I didn't go into detail, but I'm sure he caught the urgency in my voice.

I went back to Arthur, and put my hand on his shoulder. I said, "Thanks, kid," which seemed rather inadequate under the circumstances, but still showed how I felt. Then I said gently, "But you shouldn't have shot him."

He said, "You told me about Ferguson. He killed Agnes and he probably killed Ethel Brower. The instant I saw him here I understood what it meant. He intended to kill you. That's why I shot him."

I was sweating. I said, "Where did you get the gun?"

"I've carried one ever since the night someone shot at me. I have a permit."

"But to shoot someone—that way . . ."

"I think Ferguson was the man who tried to kill me."

"You didn't say a word . . ."

"I was afraid. The way he looked at me, I knew he was going to do something. Quick. And I remembered that he killed Agnes."

"You don't know that."

"He killed her, all right."

"You only think so, Arthur. It might have been Ricardo. Killing Agnes could have been a mistake."

"That's ridiculous. You can't make a mistake when one

woman is wearing a street costume and the other has on a purple evening dress."

I said, "I appreciate what you did. But, good Lord . . ."

"I'd do it again, he said tonelessly. "If I had waited it would have been too late."

I knelt beside Ferguson. He was still breathing. That could mean anything or nothing.

The buzzer sounded again. I opened the door and Max Gold came in. There were some other men with him, and a lot of people were in the hall. "We got a call through headquarters," he said sharply. "Somebody reported hearing a shot."

I moved my head toward Ferguson. Gold said, "Who did it?"

Arthur's voice was steady. "I did."

"Why?"

"He was a murderer. He was going to kill Kirk. He tried to kill me once."

Gold telephoned for the medical examiner. A patrolman in uniform came up in the elevator and was assigned the job of quieting the crowd of tenants in the hall.

Gold started firing questions at me. He was only halfway through when the medical examiner came in. He was a fat, fussy little man. He knelt beside Ferguson and started doing things. He got up after a while and said, "I can't say for sure —but I think he'll live. We'd better get him to the hospital, quick."

They phoned for the ambulance. While they were waiting Max Gold went to work on me again. He had none of the easy friendliness which had marked our conversation earlier that evening. His questions were sharp and direct. Once more the buzzer sounded. The door opened and Dana came in. She must have been told something because her cheeks were white and she looked frightened. She saw the body on the floor, and the detectives. She saw Arthur and she saw me. Gold said, "What are you doing here, Miss Warren?"

"I came to see Kirk."

"Why?"

She looked at me, desperation in her eyes. I said, "I told her I'd got hold of some information, lieutenant. I wouldn't

149

tell her over the phone. I suppose curiosity got the better of her."

Gold said, "Is that how it was, Miss Warren?"

"Yes. I came as soon as we finished the supper show."

Gold quizzed me a little more. Then he started on Arthur. His questions crackled like machine-gun fire.

The ambulance shrieked in the street outside. They brought a stretcher up and carted John Ferguson away. A detective went with him.

I stood beside Dana. I held her hand tightly.

My brain was working overtime. It worked so fast I could hear the machinery creaking. I paid no attention to what was going on all around me.

Gold finished questioning Arthur. He smiled at Dana and me. He said, "Looks like my hand has been forced, Douglas. With this thing happening like it did, I'll have to go to work on Ferguson as of now."

"You think he'll live?"

"I'd bet on it. And by the time he's able to stand trial, I'll probably have enough evidence to convict him."

"You are convinced that he murdered Agnes Sheridan?"

"Yeh. Sure."

I said, in a voice which didn't sound like my own, "You're wrong, lieutenant. Ferguson didn't kill Agnes, and he didn't kill Ethel Brower, either."

Gold said, "What the hell . . ."

I repeated, "Ferguson didn't do it."

"If he didn't," asked Gold, "who did?"

I felt sick all over. What I faced was the toughest, meanest, lousiest job I ever had.

I said, "The person you want, lieutenant—the person who killed those two women—is standing right there. It's Arthur Maybank."

XXV

THE ATMOSPHERE in the room wasn't nice. Arthur looked stunned; Dana, shocked; Max Gold, incredulous and the other detectives, as though they didn't give a damn. Me—I felt completely, utterly and colossally miserable.

Gold was doing a high-pressure thinking job. He stared at me, then at the rug, and then at me again. He said, "You sound pretty sure of yourself, Douglas."

I said, "I'm sure, all right. That's the way it's got to be."

"Of course it is." Max's voice was heavy with sarcasm. "But being just a dumb cop, I don't see why. When did you get this brain-wave?"

"Just a little while ago. I wasn't holding out on you. Until then I hadn't even considered Arthur. Once I did, everything else dropped into place. Don't get the idea I like what I'm doing. I never felt more like a heel in my life. It would be a lot more fun to pin this on Ferguson or Ricardo. But that isn't the way things are."

Gold said, "I'm listening. But so far I haven't heard anything."

He was skeptical and just a trifle hostile. I couldn't blame him. I tried to keep my eyes away from Arthur. He looked like a shock victim: dazed and bewildered. I said, "In the first place, I don't believe Arthur tried to kill Ferguson because my life was in danger. What he did was immediate and instinctive. I think it was the instinct of self-preservation at work. If he hadn't been so excited—if his aim had been straighter—he'd have eliminated the last person who represented danger to him."

Dana said, in a small, frightened voice. "You wouldn't say something like that without being sure, would you, Kirk?"

"You know me better than that."

"I don't," stated Max Gold bluntly. "And I'm not buying yet, Douglas. You gotta give me something definite."

"All right, I will. I can prove that Arthur killed Agnes. That is the one vitally important thing I'm positive about.

I know some other things, too. But not all. There are plenty of loose ends I can't tie together, but the killing of Agnes Sheridan isn't one of them."

I looked at Arthur. He still hadn't moved or said a word or protested against what I was doing. I said, "You told me, Arthur. You told me as plainly as though you had said it in so many words."

"You might let me in on it," suggested Gold. "I'm a big boy now. You can tell me things."

I said, "I'll make it as brief as possible. The night before Agnes was killed, the four of us had dinner together at the club: Agnes, Dana, Arthur and myself. We planned to go skating Monday night. We invited Arthur and he said No. He gave two perfectly valid reasons. One was that he was on duty all night. The second was that he couldn't skate and didn't want to learn.

"Remember one more thing. Arthur had been at the club many times. He knew the show schedule to the minute. He knew when Dana would go on and when she would finish. He knew that there was an exit from the club through the adjoining building. He knew that Agnes would leave her skates in Dana's dressing room during the show, and after it was over, the two girls would go through that corridor to the dressing room. To do that, they had to pass the door of the second exit. The internes at the McKinley go off duty informally every once in a while for a variety of reasons: to run across the street for doughnuts and coffee, for instance. Arthur could leave the hospital, get to the Caliente just before Dana & Ricardo finished their act, do the shooting, and get back without ever being missed. The most elaborate check-up would indicate that he had been on duty continuously."

Gold said, "I'll swallow that, but there's still something missing. You said you didn't peg Arthur until just a little while ago. You said he just the same as told you he did it. That's what I'm asking for. The clincher."

I chose my words carefully. "It was something Arthur said, lieutenant. He said it right after he shot Ferguson. He was up in the air like a kite. I was firing questions at him. I argued that he had acted too hastily. I said that the shooting might

152

have been done by Ricardo and that Ricardo could have meant to kill Dana."

"What's wrong with that?"

"Nothing was wrong with the idea. What was wrong was Arthur's answer. When I suggested that Agnes could have been killed by mistake, Arthur said vehemently that my idea was ridiculous. He said, 'You can't make a mistake when one woman is wearing a street costume and the other has on a purple evening dress.'"

Dana said, "Oh!" and I knew she had caught my point. But Max Gold shook his head. "I don't get it," he said. "I wouldn't say there was anything dopey about that remark."

"There was only one thing wrong with it, lieutenant. What you don't know is that the dress Dana was wearing is the first purple one she ever owned. She never wore purple in her life before. The dress was delivered to her apartment less than two hours before the show went on. No one could have known that she intended to wear purple. And no one who didn't actually see her that night could know that she was wearing it. The only ones who saw that dress were those who were at the dinner show. Plus one other person. That person was the man who killed Agnes."

Gold said, "Well, whaddaya know! Supposedly, Arthur wasn't there, but just the same he saw the dress. So he *was* there. Not bad, sonny, not bad. But look: Why would he want to kill Agnes? He'd been playing around with her, but he didn't know she was Ferguson's wife."

I was deadly tired. I didn't feel proud of myself. I didn't feel anything but sorrowful. I said, "You'd better handle it, lieutenant. I hate the job I've had to do, and I wouldn't want to carry it any further. Maybe Arthur will fill in the blank spaces. If I'm right, his guilt can be proved easy enough. The bullet they'll take out of John Ferguson should tally with the bullet that killed Agnes Sheridan. What's more, if Ferguson recovers—as the medical examiner seems to believe he will—he'll do a lot of talking. All he'll be interested in will be to save himself from facing trial for murder. Even the kidnaping charge wouldn't bother him, especially since we know that he couldn't be convicted of it."

Gold started talking to Arthur. He was gentle and patient.

He explained that the similarity of the two bullets and the inevitability of a straight story from Ferguson would convince any jury. He didn't hold out any hope. He just stated facts.

Arthur didn't seem to be much interested. He looked small and pitiful in his big overcoat and his hospital whites. He was like a man in a trance. He said, quietly, "Kirk is right, lieutenant. I killed Agnes just like he said I did."

"Why?"

"Because a lot of other things had happened. They kept getting bigger and more terrible. On Sunday night, Agnes and I were alone for a long time after dinner. She asked a lot of questions. Those questions convinced me that she knew all about the jam I was in and was just trying to check on it. I was desperate and half crazy." His voice broke. "I—I'd rather not talk any more. I've told you everything you need to know. I'm glad you know it. It had to end this way."

His face went blank. He didn't seem to realize what was happening to him. He didn't seem to care. Gold glanced at me and shrugged. He said, "How much more do you know, Douglas?"

"A great deal—with plenty of details missing. But, as a beginning, I'll remind you that we never understood how Ethel Brower got into my apartment. The answer to that is that Arthur had a key. He still has it. I had been away, and Arthur was using my apartment on his off nights."

Gold said softly, "Don't let me stop you."

"Candy Livingston told us that Ethel Brower knew John Ferguson. Arthur knew him, too. It was Arthur who introduced me to Ferguson.

"On January 25th, Candy Livingston's representatives gave a package containing a half million dollars in unidentifiable bills to an emissary of the person who was presumed to have kidnaped Candy. That was the night of one of the worst blizzards New York has had in forty years. The money was handed over, according to the newspapers, in Central Park, near Fifth Avenue.

"An hour or so later a man named Norton was hit by a reckless, or a snow-blinded, driver. That was also in Central Park, but it was on the West Side near the 72nd Street entrance. It's difficult to imagine anybody strolling in the park that night just for the fun of it. A passing motorist phoned for an ambulance. The call—as I understand the procedure—was routed through police headquarters to the proper precinct. The McKinley Hospital got the call. Arthur was on 'accident' and made the ambulance run. I believe there is some connection between the man who was injured in the park and Candy Livingston's ransom money. Your guess is as good as mine. Only Arthur knows the truth."

Arthur didn't wait for Gold to question him. He said, in a flat, expressionless voice, "I'll tell you about it. I haven't anything more to lose now."

He swallowed and then moistened his lips.

"That's the way it started," he said. "Just a routine call: a man who was dying. I did what I could on the spot and then rode inside the ambulance with him. He was conscious, but he knew he was dying. I picked up his belongings: his hat, one glove, a bulky package. He said there was a half million dollars in that package. He said it belonged to a man named Ferguson. He seemed terribly anxious to be assured that the money would be delivered to this man. Then he said that $100,000 of it belonged to him and that I could keep it, if I'd take the balance to Ferguson and explain what had happened.

"I didn't know it was ransom money. Of course, I suspected there was something funny about it, but I agreed anyway. The temptation was too great. You see, I've been broke all my life. Here was my chance to have some of the things I've always wanted.

"Norton died shortly after he got to the hospital. I put the package of money in my room. The next day I did just what he had told me to do. I took out $100,000 and hid it. I delivered the rest to Ferguson. He seemed satisfied.

"Several days later I read about the kidnaping and the ransom money. I should have gone to the police, but I didn't. That still looked like all the money in the world. I kept it and thought about it, and then—when I figured it was too late to tell the police anyway—I commenced to get scared. I was afraid it would be found in my possession."

I said, "So you deposited it to my credit?"

"Yes, Kirk. I didn't mean any harm. You've been my friend. I wouldn't hurt you."

I said, "I know you wouldn't, Arthur."

"I didn't dare keep the money," he continued. "I couldn't throw it away. I put it in your account. I knew you wouldn't find out about it until your monthly bank statement came in. I knew you'd tell me. That way, I'd always know what was happening—I'd know when and if the police started tracing it. I suppose I figured further than that, too. I had an idea that if nothing had happened in, say, a year—I'd invent some sort of a plausible story. I knew you'd believe me and give it back. You'd have forgotten all about dates and kidnapings and things like that."

He stopped again and I prodded him. Gently, as Gold had done. "About Ethel Brower?" I said.

"She was the sweetheart of this man Norton who gave me the money. She knew all about it. She went to Ferguson to ask for Norton's share. Ferguson told her Norton had given it to me. She came to see me and asked for her share. She wanted at least half. I told her what I had done. I explained that no matter how willing I was to give it to her, I couldn't. It was in the bank, in your name. I told her I couldn't touch it. She didn't believe me. Before she left me she said she was going to see you. I knew what she would say. I knew you were out with Dana that night. I went to your apartment and waited—just in case she showed up. When she did, we had a talk. She threatened me. She said I was in this kidnaping up to my neck. She started to call the police. I tried to stop her. I got panicky. I strangled her. She died very quietly. She looked so peaceful that I thought maybe no one would know she had been killed. I closed her eyes, turned out the light, and walked down the fire stairs. Nobody saw me."

I said, "I had wondered about her eyes being closed. That's one of the things that occurred to me after I thought it was you, Arthur. It doesn't follow that a doctor would close the eyes of a dead person, but no layman ever would."

Arthur went on talking. His voice was low and monotonous. He had been bánged around so much that he didn't care any more. "Ferguson read about Ethel Brower being killed in your apartment, Kirk. He wanted to meet you. He didn't know how far the police might go in a murder investigation. I suppose he was afraid that if they suspected me, I'd talk. He was afraid of that. He wanted to get in personal touch with you so he'd have a double check on what was happening. I shouldn't have fooled you, Kirk. I hate that worse than the other things I did."

I felt like bawling, but I kept a grip on myself. I said, "And Ricardo's luck piece, Arthur? You put that in the apartment yourself, didn't you?"

"Yes. It seemed I'd always be in danger if there wasn't some other suspect. I stole the luck piece out of Ricardo's dressing room one night when he was dancing." His eyes brightened a trifle. "And the man who shot at me: I think that was Ferguson. He was a smart man, but not very brave. When he failed to kill me, he was probably afraid to try again." He spread his hands helplessly. His head had drooped so that I could see the sparse brown hair. He was through. Finished. I would have enjoyed kicking myself around the block.

Cops are supposed to be tough, especially homicide cops. But Max Gold wasn't. He didn't like the job he had to do. He put his hand on Arthur's shoulder and said, "Maybe we better get goin', kid."

Arthur gave me a piteous smile. He said, "Don't think I blame you, Kirk. You did the right thing. You couldn't do anything else."

They took Arthur Maybank away. Everybody went away except Dana and me. We were alone with the ghost of a tragedy. Dana crept into my arms and started to cry. Then she saw that I felt worse than she did. Se went to work on me trying to cheer me up. It was a pretty futile job. I couldn't believe that I'd ever feel cheerful again.

I took Dana home and offered to spend the rest of the night in her apartment. She said No, and sent me home. My place looked awful. I hated it. I wanted to get out of there. The room was filled with too many dreadful things that I wanted to forget.

I surprised myself by going to sleep. I slept until eleven o'clock. I was awakened by the telephone. It was Dana.

She said she had phoned the office and they had told her

I wasn't there. She asked how I was, and told me she was feeling better, too. She asked whether I would drop by her apartment on the way to work.

I got there in about half an hour. Dana looked haggard, but there was a light in her eyes that made me think that something good was coming.

She sat beside me on the couch. She took my hand and put my arm around her. Her body was warm and soft. She said, "Is it wrong to be happy when we've been through so much misery, darling?"

I said that it certainly wasn't and asked her why.

She said, "Ricardo just left. I had him come over, because I thought he had a right to know. I told him everything. I never saw anybody so relieved. The police had terrified him. They had made him believe that they could convict him easily."

She looked up at me.

"He was so relieved that he was pitiful. And when he learned that you had figured it out—that you had saved him —he made the one generous gesture of his life. He said he'd give me a divorce."

This was sudden, but it was good. That made it harder to digest.

But when it did sink in, I did things. I put the other arm around her. I held her tight. I said, "Dana, sweetheart. We're engaged."

She smiled. "We've been engaged for a long time, Kirk," she said. "But now we're engaged to be married."

THE END